Good Luck,
Miss Wyckoff

Good Luck, Miss Wyckoff

a novel by
WILLIAM INGE

An Atlantic Monthly Press Book
Little, Brown and Company - Boston – Toronto

LIBRARY OF CONGRESS CATALOG CARD NO. 75-110260

FIRST EDITION

ATLANTIC—LITTLE, BROWN BOOKS
ARE PUBLISHED BY
LITTLE, BROWN AND COMPANY
IN ASSOCIATION WITH
THE ATLANTIC MONTHLY PRESS

Published simultaneously in Canada
by Little, Brown & Company (Canada) Limited

PRINTED IN THE UNITED STATES OF AMERICA

for Ellis

It is more righteous in a man that he should eat strange food and that his cheek so much as lank not, than that he should starve if the strange food be at his command.

SAMUEL BUTLER
Life And Death, Chapter 3

Good Luck,
Miss Wyckoff

I

EVELYN WYCKOFF sat on the footstool that belonged to the big overstuffed chair that Mrs. Heming kept in front of the fireplace. It was considered Mr. Heming's chair when he was home on weekends, and he would lounge in the chair reading the newspaper, listening to the little radio on the table there, and napping after meals. When Mr. Heming was gone during the week (he sold oil-well supplies), others in the family, including Miss Wyckoff and another schoolteacher, Beth Hughes, who roomed with the family, used the chair with the knowledge that they were usurping another's rightful seat. Miss Wyckoff herself had rarely sat in the chair when she used the living room of the house. Of course Mr. Heming didn't object to others using the chair, particularly when he was out of town; but Miss Wyckoff for some reason felt uncomfortable about using anything, even a piece of furniture, if she knew it was reserved for another. The chair had always seemed to her to be Mr. Heming's chair. He belonged in it, and it would have looked strange for him to sit anywhere else in the living room when he was home. So she never challenged his title to the chair. It had been her custom since she had moved in with the Hemings ten years ago to sit on the stool before the large brick fireplace when she wanted to glance through the newspaper or when she was waiting for some of her friends among the other teachers to pick her up in the evening to go out to dinner and perhaps a movie. It was strange, she often thought, how everyone continued to sit by the fireplace even in warm weather. Cold winters had made the fireplace the natural center of the house, the heart and hearth, from November through March, half the year, sometimes longer; and the rest of the year, members of the family continued to gather there by habit. Habit could be strong, Evelyn Wyckoff knew, and hard to break.

Evelyn was glad that Mr. Heming was out of town now. She had always liked him and considered him "a very nice man," but she wouldn't want to have to face him now to say goodbye. But then, no one else in the household had put in an appearance to say goodbye. If

Mr. Heming were home now, he probably would be upstairs in his bedroom with his wife, both waiting for Miss Wyckoff to leave, not wanting to have to face her now, not knowing how they possibly could face her, before her taxi came to take her to the railroad depot where she would take the train home to Belleville, leaving behind the little town she had been a part of for ten years, never to see it again. Certainly, she would never see it again.

It occurred to Evelyn that she and Beth had both felt more comfortable when Mr. Heming was gone, that neither of them had ever felt truly at home when he was there. This fact now seemed somehow not right to Miss Wyckoff. Why should grown women like herself and Beth feel that they could not comfortably remain grown women when a middle-aged man was living in their midst? Instead, they were like children suffering a loss of freedom to play at the games they liked to play when an authoritative father is present.

Miss Wyckoff held one hand to her breasts as if to soothe them now. They were greasy with the ointment she had spread on them after the burns she had incurred several days before in the last episode of a frightening relationship she had been carrying on with one of the students at the junior college. She didn't want to think about it now. She had taped gauze over the ointment to prevent it from soiling her dress. It would be healed in a few more days. And physical pain didn't hurt her the way her conscience did, full of guilt and remorse and humiliation. She mustn't think about it.

It was a warm day in early April. April weather was always an uncertain thing in Kansas. Sometimes winter would spread over into April, or spring would come early with heavy rains. But this year, April promised to be sunny and green and warm. Probably the other passengers on the train would think she was a little crazy to be carrying her mink-dyed muskrat coat with her. She refolded the coat now over her arm. It was her proudest possession. She had bought it from one of the big department stores in Kansas City, with a down payment and an agreement to pay a certain amount of money each month for a year, until the total cost was covered. It was hers now. It had been hers for two years. She had taken care never to sit on the coat but to lift it up over her hips when she wore it in a car or bus, so that the pressure of her fanny would not wear out the fur on the seat of the coat. She was very glad now that she had taken such precautions (the coat still looked good as new), for as conditions stood now, she might never be able to buy another fur coat. She might never find another teaching job anywhere in the nation.

Evelyn Wyckoff was now thirty-seven years old, and as she sat on the stool and regarded her luggage, sitting on the floor around her, she realized that every possession she owned in the world was packed into the three suitcases and the trunk. And in her handbag, too, of course. What was the saying in the Bible? "Lay not up for yourselves treasures upon earth . . . but lay up for yourselves treasures in heaven." Maybe treasures in heaven were waiting for her. She hoped so. She had few treasures on earth: her fur coat (and she admitted that she *treasured* it), a small diamond ring that had been her grandmother's engagement ring, a string of cultured pearls, two thousand dollars' worth of oil stocks that paid her a small annual dividend, and eighteen hundred dollars in the bank. Those were her treasures. And her master's degree. She treasured it because it might possibly serve to get her another job in a part of the country far enough away from this town of Freedom, Kansas, for no one to have heard of her disgrace, where she could start life over.

It was an hour before train time. She had always been an early bird. Whenever she had to catch a train, she would be at the depot a half hour before the train was due. She never planned it that way. It just happened that way. Sometimes she wouldn't realize how early she was until she got to the depot and looked at her watch and then thought to her embarrassment how futile her haste had been. But it was better than running to catch a train. She hated the anxiety of haste. And once she knew she was leaving, she wanted to get the leave-taking over with. Now she was waiting for the baggageman to come and pick up her trunk. She would have to check it through to Belleville. She decided she might as well check two of the suitcases, too. It would be more comfortable to ride on the train without all that luggage surrounding her. She'd take with her just the suitcase with her overnight things. She used her handbag in a marsupial way for toting her most personal possessions: her credit cards, and compact, and lipstick, and a little vial of whatever perfume she happened to be favoring; there were also the precious key to her safety deposit box in the bank in Belleville, and ever so many scrappy little items like theater and movie stubs, receipts for medicines she had bought and for the few dinners she had bought for guests at the Hotel Gibson, all of which she expected to get her some amount of tax deduction. The handbag was also a medicine chest, containing always a small packet of

Kleenex tissues, a bottle of tranquilizers her doctor had prescribed for her, a bottle of sleeping pills, aspirin, and a bottle of Sinutabs that would sometimes clear up a sinus congestion that always threatened her with a migraine.

Several times in the past, migraine headaches had made Evelyn so nervous and ill that she had dismissed her classes and gone home — her room at the Hemings' she had always called *home* — and gone to bed. Mrs. Heming was very considerate of her at these times. Mrs. Heming was a nice, considerate woman at almost any time, and Evelyn had always considered herself fortunate to have found a room in the home of such nice people. But Mrs. Heming had not been *nice* to her this time. She had not been insulting the way some people in town had been. She had not acted outraged with Miss Wyckoff and ordered her out of her house like a character in a melodrama. She had only withdrawn as if she hadn't known how to face her, now that she had committed an act, a private act that had inadvertently become known first throughout the high school and the junior college and then throughout the town, an act that was so far out of Mrs. Heming's realm of behavior and understanding that, Evelyn knew and understood, she could no longer even pretend to treat her as a friend, as she had always done in the past. Mrs. Heming had always been quick with her sympathy for any wrong or ailment that either of her teachers suffered, wrongs or ailments that she herself could understand. The same with Beth. Beth and Evelyn had been close friends during the years they had lived, in separate rooms, at the Hemings', and Mrs. Heming liked to call them "my girls." But even Beth couldn't pretend to understand her now. Even Beth avoided her. Not out of intended cruelty but because both Beth and Mrs. Heming no longer understood her, as it would be all but impossible for them to understand any woman of their own social status who had done what Evelyn had done.

Dear God, here came Beth now, walking up the front walk, carrying with her a stack of student papers that Evelyn knew she would spend several hours tonight grading very conscientiously. Evelyn had not expected to encounter Beth again. Usually she bowled after school was out in the afternoon and didn't get home until five-thirty or six. Well, Evelyn didn't intend to move, or hide in the kitchen until Beth made her way upstairs to her room. She'd stay right where she was and leave Beth to make the best of the situation she found herself in.

Beth Hughes came in through the front door in the

usual happy but weary way she felt upon returning home
after a day's hard work. She was humming a popular song
to herself, one that had been popular among the students,
that had been played a lot at school parties all winter.
Then she stopped upon seeing Evelyn sitting on the footstool just as if she were waiting for some of the other
teachers to drive by and pick her up to go out to dinner.

How hard they all tried to find some restaurant in the
little town that would serve them tasteful food. Usually
they ate in the coffee shop of the Hotel Gibson, or drove,
several of them in a car together, out to one of the new
motels on the highway that prided itself on having a Chinese restaurant whose food was a delightful novelty to the
people of Freedom. Both places served food that was very
satisfying to people who dined out only occasionally, but
all restaurant food had come to taste alike to the teachers
who had to depend upon it nightly. Two of the teachers
shared an apartment, and occasionally a group of them
would gather there and fix their own dinner and enjoy it,
perhaps with a bottle of wine. These times were the merriest occasions of the year, merrier than Thanksgiving;
and the home-cooked food always tasted so good to them,
they would brag to each other with every mouthful.

"Kid, doesn't this beat going to the Gibson?"

"It's absolutely delicious. Why *can't* the restaurants turn out food this good?"

"Oh, they don't use real *butter* and fresh eggs and milk. They'd lose money if they turned out a meal like this."

"Food has never tasted better to me. Honestly. Sometimes, when I walk into a restaurant here, I get absolutely sick at my stomach before I even sit down at the table."

Beth Hughes stared at Evelyn as if she had never seen her before. She was close to crying. They'd not spoken since the story about Evelyn and Rafe Collins had broken and spread over the town like a noxious gas, until it became public gossip. Rafe was a sophomore on the football team at the junior college, who worked as a maintenance man in the high school and the junior college, across the street from one another, to help him earn enough money to defray his expenses going to school. He was one of the out-of-town athletes selected by the coach on his scouting trips. He came from Bartlesville, Oklahoma, and the coach had had to promise him a lot of financial aid to persuade him to reject an offer from the University of Oklahoma. Even so, Rafe had probably chosen to come to Freedom because it was closer to Bartlesville than the town of Norman where the university was located. And

Rafe liked to be able to go home and be with his mother on Saturdays and Sundays (the games were usually played Friday afternoons).

Beth had not avoided Evelyn for reasons of moral disapproval, but because she did not know how to face her. When the story became known throughout the school, teachers and students both felt that Evelyn Wyckoff had suddenly become a different person from the woman they had known, a good teacher of Latin, beginning and advanced, more respected by students than most teachers, who was very stringent with the A's and B's she gave as grades, who had served as a responsible member on many faculty committees, and had been a forceful speaker at many P.T.A. meetings, making her audience of parents understand the need for some school policies or expenditures they had been objecting to, sometimes vociferously, because they did not see the need for them, or because they considered some of these policies and teachings "Communistic." The principal, Mr. Havemeyer, had been grateful to Miss Wyckoff many times for her courage and forthrightness at these meetings. Some of the townspeople were so terrified of Communism they had objected even to the school's prescribing any student reading on the subject. And whereas there were never any objections to the sums of money spent on athletics, citizens were critical of every penny spent for books in the library or new teaching facilities. Student morals were another topic about which Miss Wyckoff had spoken out very rationally and clearly, even though her viewpoint had now come to be used against her: "The school cannot be all things to all students," she had dared to state in a speech to parents. "We cannot be nursemaids to children who have been hopelessly spoiled or neglected in the home, nor can we fairly be held responsible for behavior outside the classroom which reflects more upon home environment and parental guidance than upon what you like to call 'moral lassitude' among the teaching body."

The statement was made at a P.T.A. meeting held during the postwar years when both the high school and the college were filled with returned servicemen, young men in their early twenties who had come back from war with a demand for sexual freedom that could not help but affect the moral habits of the younger students. One day, during those years, Miss Wyckoff had gone during her free hour out to the parking lot to pick up a book she had left in Marie Westover's car the night before when the two had gone together to dinner. Inadvertently, she had seen a college boy and girl together in the back seat of one of the parked cars, the girl lying back, her legs wedged apart by the boy's curly head, her hand gripping hard the boy's penis. Miss Wyckoff had heard of oral coition but its practice had never been a reality to her. That is, she had never believed that people, especially Americans, ever practiced the act (she was quite ready to believe that the French and the Italians did). When she saw that the boy's mouth was fastened to the lips of the girl's vagina and that there was an unmistakable ecstasy on the girl's face, her eyes closed as if she were experiencing some heavenly but censored fulfillment, Miss Wyckoff, as if with sympathetic pains, could experience enough of this joy that the girl was enraptured by to give her imagination some concept of what the experience was, enough to add desire to her curiosity. The two young people were so transported, they had no awareness that they were being observed. And Miss Wyckoff stood, a pillar of salt. She couldn't move. She then saw the boy hoist his hips up on the seat, and the girl take the glans of his penis into her mouth as if it were some foreign but succulent edible. Miss Wyckoff shivered with anxiety. Her Presbyterian background told her this was something "wrong," "depraved," and to be "condemned" by all "decent" people. Fear of being seen by either of the two young people (how would she ever face them again if they knew she had witnessed them in their lust?) forced her to move quietly away with her back to the car, and she retrieved her book and found another way back to the building and the sanctity of her classroom. But the scene left fragments of desire lurking in her very bowels that never would disappear. Every time she saw a robust young man now, she saw him in a new way, that made him both desirable and threatening. The masculine body had an entire new meaning to her now, and she began to wonder about the private practices of all the people she knew and met. Would so-and-so do a thing like that, she would ask herself about a friend or acquaintance, or even about a movie star whom she saw on the screen. The vision of what she had seen in the back seat of the car that day had opened up an entirely new world into which she both craved and feared entrance. This new craving and fear were something she had to live with and never expose even to Beth, her best friend, or to her sister Irma.

2

BETH HUGHES had always been in awe of Evelyn. She had wished, for instance, that she possessed even a portion of her moral courage. She had thrilled to hear her speak out at the P.T.A. meetings as she had done, every teacher on both faculties admiring her. Beth had avoided Evelyn mainly because she did not know how to look at or speak to a person she had greatly admired who had now become an outcast. And also because she felt she could no longer understand Evelyn. She could not understand how any woman of Evelyn's education and personal fortitude could have a love affair with "a nigger." Beth knew she should not call Rafe Collins "a nigger," but she was from Arkansas and had called black people "niggers" ever since she was old enough to talk. As a child, to have called them Negroes would have been an unforgivable affectation to her playmates. She knew that Rafe Collins was a college hero and a fine athlete, and that he was clean and even good-looking (for a nigger), and she was always careful to refer to him and to the other black students in the schools as "colored" or as "Negroes." But it was her heart that spoke, when the story about Evelyn and Rafe had first spread to the rest of the faculty and Beth was discussing it with considerable shock along with the other teachers she dined with that night at the Gibson. It was her heart that spoke then when she said, "But, girls, *why* in heaven's name would she do it with a *nigger?*" And ever since, Beth, like most of the other teachers, felt she no longer knew this woman she had once considered her best friend. She felt that she probably had never known her.

Miss Wyckoff didn't look at Beth when she came in from outside. She feared it might have been presumptuous to look at her. It might make Beth think that she, Evelyn, expected her to speak to her. So she kept her eyes averted from Beth while Beth stared at her. Then Beth finally spoke.

"Evelyn?"

"Oh, hello, Beth!" She made her voice sound totally unassuming.

"Are you leaving ... already?"

"Yes. The sooner the better, I should think. Wouldn't you?"

"Well . . . maybe." Beth lingered a moment or two, as if she wanted to say more but couldn't think of the thing to be said. Then she walked slowly past Evelyn on her way to the stairs. "Is Mrs. Heming home?"

Now there was the sound of tears in Beth's voice, and Evelyn realized she would much prefer shock or outrage to tears.

"I think she's in her room, Beth, but I've not seen her all day."

"May I ask . . . where you're going, Evelyn?"

"Home. That is, if I still have a home in Belleville. I trust I do. I'll stay with my parents a while and try to decide what to do. I don't know how I'll explain my situation to them. I'll have to make up a story. I might later join my sister in Omaha . . . if she'll have me." She managed a soft little laugh that made Beth feel more uncomfortable, for Beth could detect a chill sound of irony in the laugh. Beth had heard Evelyn speak often of her sister Irma, who taught in a high school up in Omaha. She knew they were very close. Evelyn's remark had indicated that her relationship with her own sister might now be threatened. It made Beth more sad. Still, Beth couldn't understand why Evelyn had...

"Well... good luck, Evelyn," was all she could think of to say.

"Thanks. I guess I'll need it, won't I?"

Beth didn't recognize the remark as a question. At least, she didn't try to answer. She trudged slowly up the stairs, as if a quick departure now would be rude, and as if by a lingering departure she could show the concern she felt for the woman who looked so lonely now. Beth was afraid she might really cry for her when she got to her room. It was painful to see one who had been so close to her now in such an abject position, a position that Beth could not possibly help her out of. What would happen to her now, Beth kept asking herself. "What in the world is she going to do?"

3

STILL the baggageman didn't appear. Well, there's no reason to hurry, Miss Wyckoff thought to herself. It occurred to her maybe she should go to her room and wait, that by sitting in the living room she might be keeping Mrs. Heming from coming downstairs. Mrs. Heming had not spoken with her for almost a week. That's how long it took, after she and Rafe had been discovered, broken in upon, as it were, by two of the other football-playing janitors, for the story of them to spread all over town. The very next day, Evelyn noticed a difference in the way her students behaved toward her in class. The second day, she could tell, all of the faculty had heard the story. Those who spoke to her at all did so in voices that were either very civil or full of the synthetic sympathy people sometimes affect to show that they are full of understanding. She knew better than to go to the school cafeteria for lunch that day. She walked to town for her lunch, eating the little she could stomach at the bus station in the company of transient people who could not be expected to know or care about the situation she found herself in. When she returned to the high school, there was a sign pasted beside the door to her classroom, MISS WYCKOFF FUCKS NIGGERS, the letters scrawled on white cardboard in show-card paint as scarlet as her sins. The sign terrorized her. She never before had felt the brunt of anonymous hatred, that kind of hatred that starts riots and lynchings. It created a tremor of panic. It was then ten minutes before the bell would ring for one o'clock classes to begin and students were milling through the corridors. Some of them stopped when they saw her and gathered in a circle to watch her reaction to the sign. "Oh God!" she cried to herself. "Please send some gallant man or woman to appear by my side and tear down this obscenity and rip it to shreds before the students' eyes." In all of her classes, she had two, maybe three male students who, she felt confident, besides liking her as a teacher and a person, would prove valiant enough to answer her prayer. Dick Jacobs, for instance, a junior, a straight

A student and a boy of character. Herb Laidlaw was another. She had helped both of those boys with extra work, taken pains to guide their growing, searching minds with special reading assignments in the classics that other students would never be able to digest. But no. Herb would not be able to stand up for her. He was a Negro, too, although she had never thought of him as having anything at all in common with Rafe Collins. She had forgotten he was a Negro, in their classroom relations. And probably Dick Jacobs would feel that the predicament she was in was too deep and involved for him to take a stand for her. Yes, she was positive that's what he would feel. Dick was still very young, fifteen, and probably he would be totally unable to understand her situation or how she had got herself into it. And of course his parents, devout churchgoers, would advise him to "keep out of it." Yes. She knew as a playwright knows the lines his characters will speak that that was what his father would say to him. "Keep out of it, son." And Dick was not yet old enough to act upon his own moral judgment. But, dear God, how blessed she would feel if one, just one of her students would arrive to defend her now. Since none of them did, she decided to let the sign remain. She would not honor the sign by taking it seriously enough to remove it and wad it into trash and carry it into her classroom to dispose of it in the wastebasket. Her trembling hand reached into her handbag and searched for her key ring. Her heart was pounding so that the new blood flooding her head made her dizzy and she was afraid she might not be able to fit the key into the door. The students still formed a wide circle around her, and without even looking she could feel their eyes gawking at every move she made. And she could hear their suppressed giggling. When she got the door open and rushed into the room, she felt her knees grow weak and feared, for the first time in her life, that she might faint. But she didn't. She dropped into one of the student desk-chairs and tried to collect some calm. But there was no calm to be found. She had to impose the appearance of calm upon herself while her heart continued to pound and her head reeled. Then she saw it. A small white envelope from the principal's office. She stared at it for several moments before she could bring herself to stand and pick it up, her hands still trembling. She knew what had to be in the envelope. The sight of it terrified her like doom. For she feared this truly was her doom, the end of her life. Of course Mr.

Havemeyer was going to tell her she would have to leave
her job. And where would she find another? And how
could she live if she didn't work? But before she opened
the letter, a woman entered the classroom. Evelyn recognized her as a woman she had seen occasionally at the
school, a substitute teacher, a woman who had taught in
the high school of a nearby town until she got married
and settled in Freedom. She was trying very hard to be
impersonally pleasant to Miss Wyckoff. She even managed a noncensorious smile.

"Miss Wyckoff?"

"Yes."

"I'm Mrs. Brewster. Mr. Havemeyer called me late this
morning and told me you'd be unable to handle your
classes for a while. So I've come to replace you."

"Oh."

Then she read the message on office stationery: *Dear
Miss Wyckoff: It is imperative you see me at your earliest
convenience.* Signed with a firm hand *Harlan W. Havemeyer.* Miss Wyckoff picked up her handbag, took her
fountain pen out of the desk and her new copy of *The
New Yorker,* handed Mrs. Brewster the roll book, told her
what the last assignments had been in her classes, and

then looked around to see if there were any other of her belongings she should take home with her. She could find nothing but the potted geranium.

"I'll leave you my geranium, Mrs. Brewster."

Mrs. Brewster smiled and promised to take good care of it.

Walking out of the room, Miss Wyckoff noticed the sign had been removed. Maybe Mrs. Brewster had been thoughtful enough to dispose of it. On the way to the principal's office, she felt like a little girl, with all the guilt and fear a young girl can feel when she knows she's done wrong and has to account to male authority. Friendly Mr. Havemeyer, with whom she had worked so closely and so hard in the past, now was a fearsome creature to her. She didn't know how she could possibly face him. But maybe he was wondering how he could possibly face her. His secretary and office girl, Grace Ann, looked at Miss Wyckoff solemnly when she entered from the milling corridor into the principal's outer office. She addressed her in a funereal voice. "Oh . . . hello, Miss Wyckoff. Mr. Havemeyer is expecting you. Let me ring and tell him you're here!" Miss Wyckoff waited, and then there came a polite, "You may go in now."

Mr. Havemeyer couldn't bring himself to look at Miss Wyckoff when she entered quietly. He was standing with his back to her, his hands folded behind him, like Napoleon. Still without looking at her, he asked her to sit down, which she did. The few moments of silence were filled with the solemnness of eternity. Then the troubled man spoke regretfully.

"Miss Wyckoff . . . in all my years of experience, I've never been in a position I hated as I do this. And let me add . . . I've never been at such a loss to understand human behavior . . . if the reports I've heard are true."

Miss Wyckoff thought the least she could do was to relieve his doubts. "They're true, Mr. Havemeyer."

Then he turned and looked at her examiningly, as if he had looked at her before but had never seen her. "Well, I've had enough psychology courses to realize that there must be some reasonable explanation of it, emotional, psychological, or what have you."

"I guess the reasons are unimportant now, Mr. Havemeyer."

The principal nodded his head in agreement. "Well . . . I've always felt that teachers needed more . . . more emotional outlet. Goodness knows, we're all denied many of the normal pastimes and recreations that other citizens enjoy freely. I, for example, like to drink . . . moderately. But I never let myself be seen drinking in public."

Miss Wyckoff saw no reason to respond to this admission.

"I hope this doesn't mean serious trouble for Rafe Collins, Mr. Havemeyer."

"I don't see why you should feel concern for that ornery buck, Miss Wyckoff."

"I do. What happened was as much my fault as his. I was weak and passive in what happened, but the weak and passive are probably as much to blame, when things go wrong, as the strong and aggressive."

Mr. Havemeyer didn't take a stand on this viewpoint.

"I just want him to be able to continue his education," she added.

"I don't know yet *what*'ll happen to Rafe. He hasn't shown up for classes for several days. The town's football fans are going to be mighty sore if we kick him out of school like we should, but . . ."

"Oh no. Please don't."

"Well, to tell the truth, even though there's some resentment felt toward him now, a little among students but mainly among members of the school board, I feel that the next time he makes a touchdown, anything he's done will be forgotten."

Miss Wyckoff was able to smile a little. "Yes. I suppose."

"It's an irony of our culture that the male never suffers social opprobrium as does the woman, in . . . in a situation like this."

Miss Wyckoff said, "That's true."

Mr. Havemeyer drew in a long breath, almost a sigh, and clapped his hands over his knees. "Well, Miss Wyckoff, I think you must realize the pressure on me now. You're one of the finest teachers I've had the pleasure of working with, but . . . I have to ask you to resign as of now."

"I understand. I probably should have come to you first and given my resignation, but it's all come about so suddenly, I . . . I thought probably no action would have to be taken until the end of the week."

"You'll have to leave *now*, I'm afraid. For your own good as well as mine. Some of the calls I've been getting are . . . are threatening. I never realized there were so many violent lunatics in the world."

"I've already had to meet with some of those reactions."

"What will you do now, Miss Wyckoff?"

"I've not had time to think yet, Mr. Havemeyer. I wonder . . . could you possibly give me a recommendation? Mind you, I realize what I'm asking, but . . . maybe some place far away . . . I feel quite certain that . . . I can live up to any recommendation you might give me."

Mr. Havemeyer thought deeply. "A chap I had some classes with when I was getting my master's . . . he's superintendent of schools now somewhere in New Jersey. A good fellow. Broadminded. Of course, I'd have to tell him that I had to ask you to resign and I'll have to give some truthful explanation, for if he ever found out on his own, he'd never forgive me. But I can still give you a very high recommendation and tell him that I, for one, would trust this . . . this blackout in your behavior pattern . . . not to recur."

"Oh, thank you, Mr. Havemeyer. Thank you so much." She could hardly recognize herself, she sounded so humble. The principal's kindness had moved her almost to tears. She reached into her handbag and brought out a handkerchief she dabbed at her eyes.

"Mind you, Miss Wyckoff, I can't promise that anything will come of this, but in the East, people aren't so critical of . . . deportmental problems like this, and . . . this man is a jolly, broadminded fellow, perfectly capable of under-

standing a little slipup in behavior . . . I promise you, I'll
do everything for you in my power."

"Thank you again." She still sounded pitifully humble.

"Well, I . . . I guess it's *goodbye*, Miss Wyckoff."

"Yes. I guess it is. Goodbye, Mr. Havemeyer."

". . . and I don't think I have to tell you how much I
regret all this."

"You've been very kind."

"Good luck, Miss Wyckoff."

4

UPON leaving the office, walking the six blocks back
to the Hemings' house, Evelyn felt that she would
have to kill herself. A terror had seized her, terror of feeling herself more alone in the world than she had ever
realized she possibly could be. There was no one in all
the world she could turn to now for either sympathy
(which she wanted), or advice, or help. She could not
hold much faith that Mr. Havemeyer would succeed in
getting her a job; and besides, living in the East would be
like living in a foreign country to her. She had never felt
at home in the East. She was a Midwesterner, and the
Midwest was the only part of the country she could ever
feel herself a part of. She loved Midwestern people with
all their faults, their isolationism, their flat speech, their indifference to social and political conflicts. With all these

faults, there was a sweetness she found in most of the people, and a quick friendliness, more sincere than the genteel cordiality of the South, more warm and outgoing than the sociability of New Englanders. She could not bring herself to condemn them now. She had grown up with people exactly like the people who were ostracizing her. She knew full well their social mores and she knew she had shockingly offended them. But she knew that the people in any other small town in the country would probably accord her the same treatment. Her own parents might not offer her their home for protection if they knew.

She wondered very seriously if she could face her aged parents. Her teaching career up to this time had been full of success stories for her to report to them in her letters and in her visits home on holidays: raises, prizes her students had won in state scholarship contests, compliments from the principal and the superintendent and from parents, dinner invitations to the homes of the most reputable families in town, inclusion in the ladies' bazaar of the Presbyterian church. What lie could she possibly tell them now, to explain her leaving her job at this time of year, that would be convincing? And how could she explain her situation to her sister Irma? Close and loving as they had always been, it would be a heavy strain on their lifelong devotion for Irma to be told now that her sister had had sexual relations with a young Negro. Irma would not condemn her, but she would be unable to hold on to the same perhaps idealized image of Evelyn that she had always held. Their close relationship would necessarily change. And Evelyn necessarily would have to tell Irma the truth of why she left her job before the semester ended. But perhaps she would not have to tell her that Rafe was a Negro. That would make a big difference. Irma was perfectly capable of understanding a woman's wanting to have an affair with an attractive student, even though a love or a sexual affair of any kind in Evelyn's life would be very surprising, totally unexpected, even a little shocking, to Irma. But having had an affair with a Negro man (even though a college student, Rafe was a *man,* in his early twenties, having been out of high school two years, working in a pool hall, before Coach Symonds discovered him), even though it was the only "affair" she had ever had in her life, could not help but make her seem depraved to her Midwestern contemporaries. Such moral standards were another baffling incongruity in American mores, Evelyn knew. Despite the fact that race relations had improved enormously in the years after World War II, and that some (not all) Negro students mixed with white students as equals and as friends, and despite the fact that Rafe Collins was a very good-looking young man by any race's standards, with a clean, coppery skin, and flashing white teeth that shone like porcelain when his lips uncovered them with a smile, and shoulders broad as a wall, and a long, slim trunk to his body that spread into long, strong legs that carried him with the physical ease and grace and pride of a jungle lord. But maybe it was the mere fact of his bold sexual attractiveness that placed his affair with Miss Wyckoff in a light that was so degrading to her. It was clearly a relationship unjustified by love (how could a handsome young Negro buck and a thirty-seven-year-old spinster schoolteacher pretend to be "in love"?) that unveiled in the woman a physical lust that women, at least women in responsible public positions, are not supposed to know or feel.

But Miss Wyckoff had acted upon her own personal theory of sexual relations among all races. She had wished that she could bear a baby of Rafe's just to bring into the world another strong and beautiful person. It was a religious conviction of hers that God must have intended interracial mating to be one of man's most difficult problems to solve during his life on earth. Miss Wyckoff knew that most anthropologists had arrived at the conclusion that intermarriage among the races improved the human product. And she remembered a book she had read of some popular author that explained the health and beauty of the new breed of Hawaiians, attributing this superior condition to their being a mixture of all races. The thought of this human blending seemed to Miss Wyckoff to be divine, and she was sometimes moved to tears to see evidences of love between two races. The world in another century or two should consist of only one race, the human. Most of her teacher friends had heard Evelyn espouse this philosophy, at one time or another, and some had been impressed and agreed most heartily. But those who had agreed with her had not come to her now with any warmth of understanding of her sudden frightening position in society.

By the time she arrived at the Hemings', Evelyn had decided to call Dr. Neal for a prescription of sleeping pills to be delivered, and to call a taxi to drive her out to one of the motels on the highway to Wichita where she would take a room, undress for bed, take all the pills at once and not wake up. For she felt herself not strong enough to bear her new, suddenly imposed role as an outcast in the only society she knew. She didn't want to wake up on another day in which she would have to face life in this forsaken position.

The house when she entered then was so quiet it was as if haunted. Beth was not home yet, and undoubtedly Mrs. Heming was in her room. Evelyn walked softly up the stairs to her own room, where she found a note on her dresser: *Dear Evelyn, I'm afraid I must ask you to give up your room at once. Let's please not discuss the reason. Lila Heming.* The impact of the note was like a swiftly hurled bat upon her head that made her swoon, and she dropped into a chair to keep from fainting. Only yesterday morning, Mrs. Heming had served her and Beth their breakfasts together and they had all discussed the movie *Cat on a Hot Tin Roof*, which was showing for the first time at the local movie theater. Mrs. Heming thought that Paul Newman was the best movie actor since Gary Cooper, and she had liked Elizabeth Taylor ever since she had appeared as a little girl in *National Velvet*.

"Her mother comes from around here, you know. That's the truth. Norma Spradling went to school with her over in Winfield. They were girls together. Honestly."

And she had wished her merrily a good day when she

left the house with Beth, and waved a goodbye to them from the door, smiling as happily as the housewives shown on television commercials.

Evelyn had been planning to tell Mrs. Heming that she was leaving because she knew that Mrs. Heming could not possibly let her stay on, but she was not prepared for the emotional shock it was to find the note ejecting her. If only Mrs. Heming had had the grace to wait for Evelyn to give her notice. If only she had had the courage to face Evelyn and talk with her, continuing to accept her as a human being even though the necessity of her departure would be taken for granted! The note came like the blow of a sudden amputation for which the patient has not been prepared with novocaine and sedation. The entire world seemed ripped away from her now. She sat in her room gasping for breath, a hand held over her heart, petting it like a baby to soothe it and keep it from pounding so hard. If she had the sleeping pills, she'd take them now, she thought. Then she rose and hurried on soft feet downstairs to the telephone to call Dr. Neal. He readily agreed to give her the prescription for pills, but the pharmacist at the drugstore told her their delivery boy would not be able to deliver them probably until after dinner. "Very well." Miss Wyckoff spoke in a soft, defeated voice. "I'll come down and pick them up, myself." Then she called a taxi.

Without having anticipated it, Miss Wyckoff, in agreeing to pick up the pills at the drugstore, had set up for herself a series of additional social amputations that followed one upon the other like ax blows upon a once sturdy tree. The cab driver was one of Miss Wyckoff's former students. She had flunked the boy in beginning Latin when he was a junior because he had cut the class so often he could not pass the tests or make up the assignments he had missed. He had flunked most of his other classes that year, as well. He spent most of his time in the pool hall and with the girls who worked in the coffee shop at the Gibson, girls who, it was generally known, sold themselves to men staying at the hotel and occasionally to townsmen. He now increased his earnings as a cab driver by sending customers to the girls. He grinned when Miss Wyckoff got into the cab, grinned without looking at her, but keeping his face before him. She felt a little fear when she recognized him. Should she call him by his first name as she did several years ago when he was a student? His name was Thurman, she remembered, so she gave him an unassuming greeting.

"Hello, Thurman."

"H'lo!"

He was chewing gum. He didn't deign to look at her or call her by name. His smile insinuated that he now knew himself to be as good as she, that her former position as a teacher superior to him was phony, and that he had suspected her culpability long ago.

"Would you please take me to the drugstore?"

"Which one?"

His question was impertinent. There was only one first-class drugstore in town. Two or three other stores, she knew, were prepared to fill prescriptions, but they operated more like shooting galleries at a carnival, with all their slot machines, and shelves of lurid magazines and paperback novels, and counters filled with boxed candy and toys and articles the like of which her mother would once have called gimcracks. But she had to ignore impertinence now. She had to tolerate his deprecating grin that told her, more clearly than his inadequate use of language could have, that he had heard of her disgrace and so had placed her in a new social category beneath that of the woman who had flunked him.

"Jenkins'."

Without a word, and still without looking at her, he

drove off, taking her into the town's small business district, up in front of Jenkins' drugstore.

"I'll only be a few minutes. Would you please wait for me?"

"Okay, but I gotta keep the meter running."

"Of course."

He didn't bother to get out of the car to open the door for her. She hurried out by herself and walked into the drugstore, which was filled with late afternoon customers, most of them high school students sitting in the booths having Cokes, and a few businessmen buying cigars or cigarettes. A silence fell over the store as soon as Miss Wyckoff's entrance was noticed. The students all looked suddenly self-conscious, and the few businessmen stepped aside for her with the extra consideration a gentleman shows for the condemned, or maybe with the distaste of possible contamination by physical closeness to a pariah.

"Oh yes, Miss Wyckoff," the pharmacist said, sounding as if he had been cautioned that she was coming and to be prepared for her. "Here's your prescription." And he handed it to her with dispatch, wanting to get her out of the shop as quickly as possible. Out of habit, she was about to tell him to charge it, when it occurred to her that she wouldn't be here, whether or not she killed herself, to pay the bill. So she paid the sum and hurried out to the taxi.

In her anxiety, she wondered if she should give Thurman a tip. Ordinarily, she'd have no hesitation to, but the youth had been so callous, she felt he didn't deserve even a thank you. After he stopped the taxi before the house, he leaned back against the seat, an arm outstretched over the back of the seat as if to receive a tip, so Miss Wyckoff gave him a quarter. He said "Thanks," and drove off.

Oh no! Not again. Who in all the sinful world could be so heartless as to affront her so again? No. Please, dear God! Sweet, sweet Jesus! Take the nasty scrawled words away.

Miss Wyckoff stood on the sidewalk before the house with a hand over her eyes as if to blind herself to what she had seen on the sidewalk, praying God might possibly wipe the words away and let her forget she had ever seen them. But the words were still there, in glaring white chalk, when she brought her hand away from her eyes and dared to look down again: MISS WYCKOFF FUCKS NIGGERS. Instantly she ran inside the house, into the kitchen (thank God, Mrs. Heming was still in her room), grabbed a big wad of paper toweling, soaked it with water, and ran back to the front sidewalk, where on her hands and knees she did what God had not done, and washed the letters away. She was dimly aware that two or three neighbor men drove past and undoubtedly saw her engaged thus, but she didn't have the time to pay any attention. She had to finish her job. Then, sickened, wanting to vomit, she returned inside, to the kitchen, and threw the toweling into the waste. She dried her hands and returned upstairs to her room. She opened the small package from the druggist and set the bottle of pills on her dresser. She looked at them for a long time. It would take them a half hour, maybe forty-five minutes, to end her sickness and humiliation. And why should she go to the trouble of enduring another insulting taxi ride out to a motel? She wouldn't purposely bring any shame or embarrassment to Mrs. Heming, but this was her room, she had paid her rent for it, and why should she now stop to consider the feelings of others when she wanted to die? It would be easy now to get into her own bed, take the pills, and let them do their damage upon her. Mrs. Heming and Beth would think she had gone to bed early and feel no reason for concern until morning, when their concern would no longer matter.

But she couldn't do it. She didn't hate herself enough.

Actually, she still felt some deep regard for her own person, and when it came right down to it, she couldn't possibly destroy a being she still respected and loved. She set the pills in a drawer. She would take a couple at bedtime to ease her pain, and the tension she had lived with the past few days, and to help her to get a little sleep. Sleeping pills, it occurred to her, gave us small samplings of death's comfort. But she could never commit suicide. She was not genuinely sorry for what she had done. She felt no true shame for having let Rafe Collins use her as he did, for she saw that what had happened was inevitable. And she wouldn't now want to be without the experience he had given her. Even if experience cost her her job and her acceptance by society, she would choose experience if it added importantly to her personal fulfillment. And her experience with Rafe had done this.

All these thoughts going through her mind as she sat on the footstool in the living room, Evelyn wondered if, in a few years maybe, they might all become memories that she could live with. There were footsteps on the front porch. The baggageman, finally. Evelyn got up to let him in.

5

M ISS WYCKOFF did not realize who Rafe Collins
was when he entered her classroom in the late
afternoon the first day after the Thanksgiving vacation and
began to sweep the floor and wash the blackboard and
gather the dusty erasers. The football players who had
been given jobs on the school maintenance force were not
expected to start their work until after the football season
had ended. Actually, their jobs were tokens that they were
not expected to fulfill very conscientiously, tokens that
made their salaries acceptable to the school board and the
taxpayers. Miss Wyckoff had never been a football fan,
and like many other teachers she had become annoyed at
times by the requests that came occasionally from the
principal's office to accord some special consideration to a
football player, to overlook an absence or to give him a

special makeup test for one he had failed. Sometimes it seemed to her that the entire school and the whole broad field of education were reduced to a background for a heralded, winning football team. And Rafe played on the junior college team. Miss Wyckoff, even though she had her master's, taught only in the high school. She was seldom aware of the college students.

But she remembered having heard talk about the athlete when having her lunch at the faculty table. It was conceded by everyone that he was good-looking. This compliment was paid him unconditionally, without the addition of "for a Negro." And Evelyn finally did remember having seen him once or twice carrying a tray to one of the tables for two that he would occupy alone. For he behaved with an innate superiority even to the other athletes, all of whom ate their lunch in the cafeteria because the school had given them meal tickets to help them financially. And they had their own table, too, where it was taken for granted that they wanted their own company at lunch. Rafe never joined them. It may have been that, once having experienced rejection from integrated society, he chose never to risk the humiliation again and to make it appear that he was rejecting the white and

the more amenable Negro athletes by choosing the dig-
nity of eating alone.

It seemed natural to Evelyn, when she later had time to
think about the matter, that Rafe should travel so much
of the time alone. Men of physical power and beauty
are rarities in the human race, and cannot but be regarded
as divergent from the norm of human appearance as the
freak or the deformed. And such physical beauty in a
member of a minority race so long regarded as "inferior"
could not help but isolate Rafe even more. But he re-
fused to allow his physical attributes to humble him. He
knew what an impressive human being he was and he
didn't let others forget it. He bragged openly about his
looks and his athletic accomplishments, thus depriving the
other athletes from whatever pleasure they might take in
congratulating him on "a good game" or "a damned fine
play." They figured, "If the sonuvabitch is gonna congratu-
late hisself all the time, I'll be damned if I'm gonna do it."
The other Negro athletes felt exactly as did the whites.
The feeling against Rafe Collins was personal.

Girl students were always a little embarrassed in Rafe's
presence, for he looked like a boy whom any girl would
like to date; and yet, there was the disturbing fact that

he was a Negro, and being a Negro, could not be looked upon by any small-town white girls as a prospective lover or husband. Some of the girls in the junior college, when they saw Rafe Collins, probably regretted the social disapproval of miscegenation. But whatever they felt or thought they kept to themselves, and never discussed his attractiveness except with the most detached objectivity. And they avoided being around him because it was difficult to be within his physical radius without feeling the animal attraction of his body. Rafe probably mistook their diffidence for rejection. And Rafe was scornful of the half dozen or so Negro girls in the college, plain-looking and domesticated, disliking him for his arrogance. So actually, the lordly, proud Rafe Collins was undoubtedly the loneliest young man in Freedom. And although he affected a smiling good nature as he sauntered down the corridors of the school buildings or went from one room to another to do his janitor work, the heat of his hatred lay deep inside him, like a banked fire that can be brought to flames in an instant.

Miss Wyckoff was sitting at her desk when Rafe entered, wearing the one-piece coveralls of a blue-striped cotton material that were the uniform of the maintenance men. She was grading test papers in the quiet of the afternoon,

after classes were over and the building was empty of
students. She looked up when Rafe came in and said
hello and went on with her work. She noticed his presence and that he had a flashing smile when he returned
her greeting. It even occurred to her that the smile was
perhaps a little cunning. But it didn't occur to her that
she would ever become aware of the young man as anyone but the young man who cleaned her classroom in the
afternoon. Nevertheless, she became increasingly aware
of Rafe as he leisurely did his work, moving about the
room, shifting the student desk-chairs back and forth
in order to sweep under them, with a grace of movement
so silent and unobtrusive that Miss Wyckoff, still at her
work grading papers, felt herself coming under the spell
of the athlete's quiet but unproclaimed domination of the
square, white-walled classroom. He would hum softly as
if to himself, unconsciously. The sound was luring but
it destroyed Miss Wyckoff's concentration. It annoyed
her, too. He should know better than to sing in her classroom while she was trying to work. She was about to
speak to him, to ask him please to stop, but she had that
common reluctance among whites to speak in any way
censoriously to Negroes whom she didn't know well,
as she knew her own Negro students, most of whom she

had the same easy, unselfconscious communication with that she shared with white students. There were a few surly black students, of course, with whom she had given up having any kind of communication whatever. But then, there were white students just as defensive and resistant. Rather than speak to the young man now, she would speak to his boss the building superintendent, and ask him please to order his helpers not to sing on duty.

"Beg pardon, Miss Wyckoff, I din mean to disturb you with my vocalizing."

His sudden consideration disarmed her. She found herself saying, "Oh no. No. Of course not. You have a lovely voice."

It was not what she should have said. But it was true that his humming was "lovely," melodious. If she had no work to do, she could listen to him with unconcerned pleasure. It was flattering, too, that he knew and called her by name. Of course, her name was printed beside the classroom door, so it didn't take much effort for him to find it, but the mere fact that he had taken the trouble to call her by name was surprising. She looked up over her reading glasses at the young man, standing now in the center of the room moving chairs about. The buttons of his coveralls were unfastened down to his tight-

belted waist, slim and hard as a shield, and she could
see the broad span of his hard brown chest. And his
sleeves were rolled up above the hard balls of his biceps.
Was he deliberately exhibiting himself, she wondered. But
she wondered without being critical. Since the war, male
students had all been more exhibitionistic of their bodies,
as if they were competing with girls in exposing their
physical attractions, wearing tight pants and jeans, and
T-shirts like upholstery over the sometimes impressive
form of their torsos. She had never before lived with an
awareness of male buttocks or hard, flat bellies and vo-
luptuously muscled arms and thighs. She had traveled
abroad and visited museums in Paris and Rome and Flor-
ence, but the male bodies she had seen in ancient sculp-
ture she did not relate to living men. Probably it was her
intention not to. Several times she had had to ask male
students, when she found them lounging at their desks,
their legs sprawled wide apart in front of them, to sit up
straight; for she had found herself unable to avoid
glancing at the signs of maleness they seemed to be con-
sciously, perhaps purposely, displaying. She had not imagined these signs of new behavior among her male students; she had discussed them with some of the other
teachers. And it was a laughable story that spread over

both schools that one G.I. in the college, who was flunking the freshman composition class of a man who was gently effeminate, had sat in the first row in order to display himself more boldly before the instructor, intending thereby to show that he had other qualifications for getting a passing grade in the course, in case the instructor wanted to make use of them. He had openly confessed this behavior to other students, boasting that "queers" were always attracted to him. He had passed the course with a C minus, but if the effete instructor, named Chester Rollins, had taken advantage of the young man's offer of himself, no incident was ever made of it; and Mr. Rollins, a year or two later, finished his Ph.D. and got a job in a big Midwestern university.

6

MISS WYCKOFF was on the verge of a nervous breakdown when Rafe Collins first entered her classroom. Her doctor in Wichita called it "a walking nervous breakdown," inasmuch as she managed to go on doing her work and avoid hospitalization, which she could not have afforded, anyway. She could not have afforded giving up her job, either, for it would have meant a period of six or seven months, during the worst of her illness, without pay and without health insurance that covered nervous or mental ailments. And her doctor told her she would recover faster if she kept on with "life as usual." And she had had no choice but to "keep on" and do her work as best she could, although there were times when she suffered such acute claustrophobia in her classroom, she feared she would scream out against her students; and she would have to excuse herself from them, upon occasion, to go to the faculty women's lounge and take a tranquilizer. And there were mornings when she woke with such a fury of anxiety she had to squeeze the courage out of her soul to help her enter the classroom and face her students.

The trouble had begun with deep depressions that she could not account for. She could find no rational reason for them in her life. At first, she had found she could talk a little about the depressions with a few of her closest friends, Beth being one of them. And then they became so painful she didn't mention them. She began to withdraw from the casual social life she had previously enjoyed with the other teachers, and from appearing publicly in a crowd. Usually she would go home immediately after her last class was out in the afternoon and go to bed, sometimes without her dinner, for she had become repelled by food. Beth and Mrs. Heming became concerned. They talked about Evelyn between themselves, in soft, troubled voices.

"Beth, something's wrong with her, don't you think?"

"Yes, I do, Mrs. Heming, but I don't know *how* to help her. I tried and I tried to coax her last night to go to bridge club, but she wouldn't. And two weeks ago, she told Mr. Havemeyer that she simply couldn't face going to the P.T.A. meeting."

"I wonder *what* could be the matter?"

"I just wish I knew so that I could help."

"She's too young for a change, surely."

"I should think so."

"I'm probably ten years older than she is, and I haven't had *my* change yet," Mrs. Heming boasted.

"I remember, my mother had a terrible time."

"I think she should see a doctor."

"I do, too, Mrs. Heming. I'll tell her if you will."

"I guess we'll have to. I can't let her stay on like this. It's too upsetting to the household. She casts gloom in every room. I want to help her, but I can't let her turn my home into a wailing wall."

"Of course not, Mrs. Heming. You know, it's really self-ish of Evvie to be so inconsiderate."

So, each in her own way, the two women very cautiously gave Evelyn their advice. It had already been in Evelyn's mind to go to see Dr. Neal. She had resisted thus far because Dr. Neal was young, still under forty, and a romantic figure to women in Freedom even though he was married and a father. She liked him and knew he was a good doctor, but somehow he reminded her of all the handsome fraternity boys she had known in college who seemed to live totally apart from her own world of eye-strain and study. Boys who had driven around the campus in little sports cars, boys who wore expensive sweaters and slacks and sport shoes, who dated the pretty sorority girls with whom Evelyn felt she had nothing at all in common. She had watched these carefree people while she was working her way through college. She always had to pass the Pi Phi sorority house on her way from the campus to her dormitory, where she lived with about two hundred other girls, most of whom were as plain as herself. And she still had glorified memories of good-looking boys with blond wavy hair and manly tans, sitting in a little red Porsche waiting for Debbie to come out, or Sue, or Betsy. They all had such cute names. And Debbie, or Sue, or Betsy would come running out of the front door, wearing maybe a soft cashmere sweater and skirt, or a smart tweed suit of the simplest design, and cry out a happy greeting like: "Hi, Terry!" or "Hi, Ron!" The boys always had cute names, too. And the girls would jump into the little red car and off they would go to have a Coke together at the Blue Mill or one of the drive-ins where they would meet other students like themselves, and talk about fraternity parties, or the last football or basketball game, or maybe a movie. And she knew, too, that sometimes the boy would drive his little red sports car out to some remote woodsy place where he and Debbie would "neck."

These represented the blessed people of the world who were born without care, to enjoy life and all the creature comforts nature and money could provide. She felt a painful envy of them. She herself did not choose to be an A student, a Phi Beta Kappa, an honored drudge. She was these things because they were the only goals she could see that life offered her. But she dared not show her envy. In the company of the handsomely favored fraternity and sorority students in her classes, she always behaved with hauteur (she could see now that it was purely defensive and *silly* of her) that, although she was powerless to *offend* or *insult* people with such gracefully balanced egos, could not help but alienate them from whatever social intercourse might have developed between them and herself. It still embarrassed her to remember how foolishly she had behaved at times in the classroom company of these gilded people. She would address one of her own friends in French or Greek, and, her head high in the air, refer with feigned casualness to the novels of Proust or Dostoevski. Once in a while she would find one of the gilded people to be as excellent a student as herself, and this daunted her. It wasn't fair. She had reconciled herself to all the possessions and advantages they took for granted in their lives that she could not. It was as out of character for one of them to make an A plus in a difficult course as it would have been for herself to have appeared as the belle of a fraternity party.

But kindness and consideration for her health and well-being were all the sweeter coming from Dr. Neal, a man who had been a member of the enemy camp, so to speak, when she was in college. And they actually had been to college together, their undergraduate days at the university overlapping by two years, Dr. Neal having been a junior when Evelyn Wyckoff entered as a freshman. She remembered him well, but was certain he did not remember her. He never paid any attention to the girls who lived in Slocum Dorm. Not Tom Neal. Besides being a good student, he was a star basketball player and track man. And girls were very attracted to him. After getting his B.A., he had entered the medical school and taken his internship at the University Hospital in Kansas City, Kansas. Evelyn, after finishing her B.A. *summa cum laude,* transferred to the State Teachers' College at Emporia to get her M.A. Dr. Neal had been prac-

ticing a year in Freedom when she arrived there for her
first job (after a year of practice teaching in the Emporia
High School). He had entered his father's office to take
over most of his now aging father's practice. He and his
wife were members of the Freedom Country Club and
played golf and went to the country club parties, and
entertained all the socially graceful people of Freedom
in their handsome ranch-style home (with a swimming
pool) about a mile in the country outside of Freedom.
Mrs. Neal was a beautiful woman from Topeka whom
Tom had met in his undergraduate years. She had a
mink coat, and a lovely big emerald ring, and wore the
"smartest" shoes, Evelyn thought, that always looked
new, so trim and unscuffed, the heels never worn lop-
sided, the leather never bulging from the pressure of the
big toe. Miss Wyckoff had decided that smart, trim shoes
represented the well-dressed lady more than any other
article of clothing, and herself had spent as much as she
could afford on high-quality footwear of lizard skin or
suede (for dress), or dull-finished kid. She was proud of
her feet, too. They were small and well shaped, with still-
high arches.

Miss Wyckoff was a little shy of seeing Dr. Neal the

first time she came down with the flu after coming to Freedom. But Mrs. Heming insisted he was the best doctor in town.

"These young doctors know all the latest remedies. You couldn't find a better doctor than Tom Neal in Wichita or Kansas City."

And as soon as Dr. Neal entered her bedroom at Mrs. Heming's, a friendly smile on his face, an easy confidence in his presence that could not possibly be the product of simulation, a radiance of health and intelligence and vigorous life about him, Miss Wyckoff fell in love. He took her temperature, felt her pulse (her hand so small in his), looked down into her throat, asked matter-of-factly about her bowel movements, listened to her cough, and then announced still with a good nature that did not belie the seriousness of illness: "Yah! You've got it!"

"What, Dr. Neal?"

"Asian flu. There's a lot of it going around now. Better take care of yourself for a week or two. Stay in bed now until you get rid of that fever. I'm going to give you a shot of penicillin, and call Jenkins' for some pills to be delivered, and if you're not better by day after tomorrow, I'll be by again. But you're going to feel lots better then, I think, and you can drop into my office at the end of the week."

"Oh, thank you, Dr. Neal." She felt as if one of King Arthur's beautiful knights had come to minister to her. How nice he was! How foolish she had been to be shy of the man! How lifted her heart was to have been accorded such friendly therapy.

"I believe we were schoolmates together at K.U.," he said while packing his stethoscope into his bag, and his thermometer, and his hypodermic syringe.

"Why . . . yes. Yes. We were. I remember you so well playing basketball." (She had never once attended a basketball game. For one reason, the tickets cost money that she needed for other things.) "And track."

"Oh yes," he bantered, "I was quite the athlete in those days. I'm glad now. Competitive sports do a lot for a young man, not just in physical fitness but in developing character, I believe. You know, the most important thing that sports ever gave me was the grace to know how to lose." Then he smiled. "It really takes a man to accept defeat." He wished her well again and left, saying goodbye to Mrs. Heming downstairs (Miss Wyckoff could hear) on his way out.

"To lose," Miss Wyckoff thought. "To accept defeat." Did such a man really know what it meant to lose? As she herself had lost, or felt she had lost, something essential to life? She wondered about the vague feeling of loss she had lived with for as long as she could now remember. What was it? Was it only something as simple as a husband and children and a home? She knew many women who had these but were miserable and led lives that were totally meaningless, or harmful to others. But she felt as if she had lost something very precious in life. Precious to herself, and possibly precious to others. Regardless of how hard she worked at her teaching, or how conscientiously she graded the students' papers and conferred with them to sharpen their intelligence and give them knowledge, she felt as if she had always withheld some vital part of herself from the world and the people she loved.

Depression finally overcame Miss Wyckoff, early in the school year in which her life later became involved with that of Rafe Collins. After the few hours of sleep she would get at night, she would awaken early in the morning with a despair so overpowering she couldn't fight it. Finally she gave up trying to go back to sleep when she wakened at four A.M., or sometimes at three. Mrs. Heming had given her permission to use the kitchen when she

got up in the morning. She would put on her flannel robe
and her pink satin mules (how foolish they looked to her
now! What idiocy had ever possessed her to buy such friv-
olous, impractical slippers!) and make her way down
the dark stairs to the kitchen and put the water on for
her coffee. She would drink three or four cups to bolster
herself. Sometimes she would drink so much, it turned
bitter in her stomach and made her nauseated. Then she
would try to ignore her almost hallucinatory fears by
grading papers or making lesson plans. Sometimes the
effort was too great and she would be able only to sit
with the evil company of her hopelessness. It seemed to
her now that she had no life whatever, that in her teaching she was only playing at having a life, as a child
would play at being an adult by playing house. Nothing
she had ever done in her life seemed now to have any
worth or meaning. Her master's thesis, her years of hard
study, her ten years of teaching, the few summers of work
she had done at Columbia on her Ph.D. Only her memories of childhood still seemed real to her. Her life since
then had no substance nor reality. She was a total failure.
She wished to God that He would take her life, but that
was useless, too. As useless now as praying. She felt totally alien to the world, as if she were not a functioning

part of it, and alien to God, Who had forgotten her existence. Finally she had to give up trying to teach her classes. She began staying at home, most of the time in bed. When she did get up, her silky reddish hair was left to hang over her shoulders and down her back. Her face, without makeup, was often not even washed. She began neglecting to bathe. Usually now she went about her room and even came downstairs barefoot. And then Beth and Mrs. Heming began to hear her at night cry out in her sleep, cries that sounded like cries from hell's most tortured souls.

She had protested the other women's pleas for her to make an appointment with Dr. Neal.

"What good can he do? He's a physician. There's nothing wrong with me physically. I'm going mad. I know I am. I'm going mad."

"Just go down and talk to him, Evelyn. I know he's just a physician, but he'll be able to tell you where to go to seek whatever kind of help you need."

Some of her pride returned when she was finally persuaded to call for an appointment, and Beth helped her get dressed to go downtown to appear in his office. But what a humiliation for her to appear so abject before a man she so admired. It was more than admiration; it

was a crush she had on him, a secret, schoolgirl crush.
And she would have liked to appear at country club parties as his social peer. She had often fancied herself at one
of the Saturday night dances (she had never attended
one but had heard gossip from the plainer people in town
about the way "the society folks" behaved at the club),
wearing a risqué dress like one she remembered Norma
Shearer wearing in a movie years ago, a dress that would
reveal her soft, white neck and shoulders, which she knew
were as beautiful as those of any woman alive, by far her
best feature (she regretted that the rest of her body was
a little stocky, although she had lovely slim ankles and
wrists), with her silky reddish hair all swept to one side
of her head leaving one ear naked, adorned by a pendu-
lant earring that fell to her shoulder. She would approach
Dr. Neal and his wife Bobbie with a worldly smile and
joke with Bobbie that she was going "to *steal*" her husband from her "for just one dance."

Most of the gossip about country club parties centered
on marital infidelity, wives sneaking away from the dance
floor with other women's husbands and vice versa. There
had even been gossip that Tom Neal was having an affair
with the beautiful widow Fern Hudson, who had been a
threat to other wives in Freedom ever since her husband

had been killed in action in the South Pacific. It hadn't always been country club wives she threatened, either.
There had been whispered stories about Fern Hudson and
some of the lowlier men in town, one of them a handsome
young Italian grocer, and one a ballplayer from Oklahoma
who came to Freedom every summer to play on their
team, the Freedom Fighters, until one of the major league
teams picked him up and took him away to national
fame. It was difficult for her to believe that a gallant
man like Dr. Neal would be unfaithful to such a sweet
and pretty wife as Bobbie, but she knew, from literature
if not from life, that men's ways are often disillusioning,
and women's ways (like Madame Bovary's) often cul-
pable. And Mrs. Hudson had become a legend in town
for her beauty and her reported romances with men
whom less daring women would never dream of having
personal relations with. Miss Wyckoff had always secretly
admired Mrs. Hudson for being so beautiful (and much
older than she looked) and so cavalier as to flout public
opinion. People will forgive a beautiful woman almost
anything, Miss Wyckoff philosophized. Occasionally she
had encountered the celebrated beauty at Clark's, the
only chic ladies' shop in Freedom. Mrs. Hudson would
smile upon her almost benignly, and once had noticed a

book that Miss Wyckoff was carrying, a copy of the poems of Dylan Thomas.

"I believe I read something about that book in *The New Yorker.*"

"Oh, he's a very great poet," Miss Wyckoff had managed to mutter. (Why was she so shy and defenseless in the company of physical beauty and social gracefulness?) She had tried to convey some impression of the beauty and excitement of the poems, for Miss Wyckoff loved literature, and had minored in English at the university, having a hard time deciding which she really preferred to teach, English or Latin. It was probably a streak of snobbishness in her that made her elect the classical language, she thought now, because (in her opinion) anyone could teach English.

She noticed that as she talked about the beauty of Thomas's poetry Mrs. Hudson's face was becoming expressionless.

"I could never enjoy poetry," Mrs. Hudson replied without apology, leaving Miss Wyckoff speechless. She could not imagine life without poetry. But how she admired Mrs. Hudson for the casual bravery she showed in admitting that she did not like poetry, for Miss Wyckoff had found that the dullest souls, incapable of any aesthetic responses, would at least profess to a liking of poetry. Women of Fern Hudson's beauty and financial security (Jim Hudson had been the scion of one of the wealthiest families in Freedom) didn't have to profess anything they didn't truly feel or believe. Maybe Fern Hudson's life (with her reported love affairs, that sounded very romantic to Miss Wyckoff) contained poetry, and therefore she didn't have to seek it in literature. It was a personal observation of Miss Wyckoff's while she was still in college that people who live active, romantic sex lives have little or no interest in reading about such experiences. And why should Fern Hudson, who spent her nights between satin sheets with naked lovers, and her days at luncheon parties, or bridge games, or golf, or riding, why should she ever bother to read anything at all? Yet, Miss Wyckoff regretted that Mrs. Hudson didn't like poetry. She'd like to think of her as a kind of Pompadour or Maintenon who showed as much perception in politics and literature and the arts as in her love affairs. But the aristocracy of Freedom, Kansas, was not that of eighteenth-century France.

Miss Wyckoff could not help but wonder to her own discredit how much of her own aesthetic hunger was only a sublimation (that's the word Freud would have used) of her uneventful love life, her busy brain trying to compensate for all the experiences life had never granted her. Or maybe it was unfair of her to blame life. Probably she could only blame herself for her reluctance to become an active part of life, her fear of it, like that of a wallflower at a ball, holding her from being an active participant. She feared that life had come to her only in predigested forms, history books, novels, poems, and plays. And she had come to regret this.

Miss Wyckoff was pained that she had to visit Dr. Neal now with only her misery and hopelessness to convey to him. Beth accompanied her to his office and sat there reading an old copy of *Life* magazine when the gallant doctor ushered Evelyn into his consulting room.

"Now what seems to be the trouble, Evelyn?" It made her feel better just to hear him call her by her first name. Already she could respond to the man's warmth and concern for his clients, which seemed now to be especially reserved for her. This warmth and concern, like magic, released the tension and self-pity that had been storing up inside her for weeks. She had so successfully repressed her emotions, she could never have expected herself to react as she did to the doctor's simple question, asked in such a friendly voice. Before she could utter a word, Miss

Wyckoff collapsed in shuddering tears, her body heaving with the gasping breaths she sought to support her hysterical outburst. Dr. Neal sat by patiently until Miss Wyckoff was able to talk. She tried to convey to him some of her misery of the last several weeks, but words had never been so elusive or inadequate. How could she possibly describe the despair which wakened her every morning, that made the sunshine look idiotic, and each morning greeting addressed to her sound like bitter mocking?

The only concrete evidence that she could give him of her illness was to describe the uncertainty of her periods, her loss of sleep, and of appetite, and of interest in any of her friends or anything that happened. "I can't even sit still to enjoy a movie, Dr. Neal. I can't find anything to take my mind off myself."

"Those are the usual symptoms," he answered solemnly. "Have you always been inclined to depressions?"

"Not like this. I mean . . . I've always been what I guess you'd call *moody*, but . . ."

"Tell me more about missing your periods."

"Oh, I promise you, I'm not pregnant. I couldn't possibly be. I . . . I've not had sexual intercourse . . ." Then she added lamely . . . "for a long time."

Dr. Neal looked at her scrutinizingly, and rubbed his chin. "How old did you say you are?"

"... Thirty-five."

Then as though to himself, "I wonder."

Eager, "*What?*"

"You say you've missed some of your periods."

"Yes. Two in the past several months, but not consecutively."

"Well, first let's give you a thorough physical, Evelyn," he said in an everyday voice that comforted her more, giving her the confidence that she was being treated and attended to. "It's just a routine thing to do, but sometimes these emotional upsets have their cause in something organic. Now if you'll step behind this screen, you may undress. Miss Bullit will help you." He called his nurse in from the reception desk to hang up Miss Wyckoff's clothes and give her a white linen smock to wear back into the consulting room. Miss Wyckoff could not help but think of the false modesty of putting on a smock just to wear until she lay down on the examination table totally naked. It seemed an inconsistency like that of the artist's model who, after posing naked, modestly dons a robe during the rest periods. Apparently the naked body was offensive except when nakedness served a purpose or function.

If she had not been a patient, Dr. Neal might have commented upon Miss Wyckoff's milk-white flesh as she lay naked upon the table before him; and had he been more aesthetically inclined, he might have compared her plumpness and fine features to a Holbein. But he said nothing as he probed her body with his strong fingers which Miss Wyckoff had admired, noticing the gouged cleanness of the broad nails. When she saw him draw a rubber glove upon one hand and casually lubricate his middle finger, she felt a little dread, guessing what he meant to do. So she automatically parted her legs to enable him to insert the finger into her vagina. She could not help but notice a look of repressed surprise upon his face when his finger was blocked from total entry. She held her breath, remembering her false implication that she had had sexual experience in the past. She was humiliated now by her maidenhead. She was panicked for him to discover her a virgin. It made her feel a failure, a failure as a woman, to be virgin at the age of thirty-five. Withdrawing his finger, Dr. Neal said gravely, concealing his surprise, "I'm afraid I'll have to ask you to turn over on your stomach, Miss Wyckoff." (Why had he suddenly decided to drop the familiar appellation? She felt he had done so to withdraw anything personal in their relations.)

She complied and he placed one hand on her dimpled buttock, pulling the loaf of soft flesh aside to enable his finger to enter her anus, which, her vagina forbidding entrance, would enable him to feel the condition of her ovaries.

"I'm afraid this is going to hurt a little. I'm sorry." And it did hurt. He was probing apertures in her body that had never been forced into expansion by young men's excited fingers or swollen cocks, but had remained tight-fitting doors to the unentered vaults of her body. Dr. Neal probed inside her and then withdrew his slick finger without committing himself, but keeping what Miss Wyckoff could not help but feel was a mysterious silence.

The examination continued in silence for almost an hour. Then he drew a sample of blood from a vein in her arm, gave her a shot of vitamins and another of hormones (she dreaded each time the prick of the needle); and then he told her to put on her clothes, that he would talk with her. His manner, she thought, concealed some terrifying knowledge he had found of her. She dreaded the talk more than the examination. She knew that he was going to tell her things she would rather perish than have him know.

"Miss Wyckoff, did anyone ever tell you you're an attractive young woman?" This was his first question after she was dressed and seated beside his desk.

She had to think hard, back into the past, in order to answer his question. No. No one had ever told her that. But she shook her head for an answer. She was afraid to use the delicate instrument of her voice which might crack with self-pity and give away her cringing humiliation.

Dr. Neal went on. "Now please don't think I'm one of those doctors who tell their patients that all's the matter with them is the need for a little romance. No. I'm not a psychiatrist, but I know enough about the field of emotional disorders to say that sex alone is not a remedy for *any*thing . . . And yet . . ." Now he was trying to get up the nerve to say something it was very difficult to say. "Yet, nature meant us to *use* our bodies, Miss Wyckoff. If we don't, they dry up on us and begin to function poorly."

"I'm in good physical health, am I not?" she asked a little defensively.

"Generally, yes. Very good health. Heart and blood and liver and lungs. But . . ." and again he hesitated.

"Is it a crime to be a virgin, Dr. Neal?"

"Well . . . perhaps to nature, it is. At least, after we have reached a certain age." He paused again. "Have you ever been in love, Miss Wyckoff?"

She thought hard. No. She had never been truly in love. She had had crushes on a few attractive boys when she was a girl, and later on a few movie actors or handsome men she happened to meet, and now upon the doctor himself. She shook her head, still not trusting the sound of her voice. And she kept from looking at the doctor. She sat with her head dropped down, like a woman condemned.

"I know it's a hard life for you unmarried teachers here in Freedom. They don't allow you much privacy, and your personal lives are always open to criticism, but . . ." Again he paused.

"You think it would help me to have sexual intercourse. That's what you're trying to tell me, isn't it, Doctor? I can understand your reticence."

"I recommend it if you find a man you're fond of. Yes. But it should be a happy relation, and I'd hate to see you feeling worry and guilt about being discovered. For it *could* cost you your job, as you yourself probably know. But I'm certain if things were managed discreetly . . . Maybe you could meet someone in Wichita, or . . ."

"I can't think that the terrible depression I've been feeling can be cured by . . . by a romance, Doctor. For one thing, I feel totally incapable of romantic feelings . . . toward *any*one. I . . . I'm such a novice, I wouldn't know how to look for a romance or how to behave in one. That's the truth, Dr. Neal. I . . . I've always had a terrible fear of . . . of the sexual experience. Don't ask me why. Problems of early environment, I suppose. But I can't go into those problems here." Her virginity having been discovered, she could now discuss it thus freely.

"No. This isn't the time or place. Of course you don't feel like a romance now. You won't until your depression begins to lift. And I'm going to send you to a psychiatrist in Wichita. He's a very good one, you may take my word for it. Came out here from the East a few years ago. A Jewish man. I hope you have no antagonism to Jews."

"Oh good heavens, Doctor. I have no racial prejudices at all. Everyone who knows me knows how I've fought at the school for equality and . . ."

Her voice ended when the doctor spoke, lightly, dismissing the liberal viewpoints she was so proud of. "Very well. I'll give you his name and address, and I'll call him myself to apprise him of your call."

"Is he terribly expensive? "

"I think he'll manage to fix a price within your budget."

"I hope so."

She watched him as he wrote out the doctor's name and address, and some prescriptions. How beautiful he looked to her! What a noble head! And how finely made, with his well-kept hands, and his still athletic body, and his expensively tailored trousers pressed with a sharp crease, and black shoes with a gloss like enamel. Why was it that men in the field of education never had the look of being tailored and groomed that Dr. Neal and some of the businessmen in town wore so naturally? His cotton jacket, the sleeves now rolled up above his wrists, was white and starched, with a tailored look, too. Miss Wyckoff noticed the smooth black hair on his forearms, which aroused her sensually. She would never have feared the sexual act with a man like this one. What an irony that she should be told by this man, whom she could love and give herself to with abandon, that a sexual experience would be therapeutic to her condition. Then why couldn't he have made love to her, and inserted his fine penis into her body instead of all those needles? But that would have been against his professional ethics. And besides, she was not sufficiently confident of her womanhood to expect a man like Dr. Neal to love her. She was not Fern Hudson, or Bobbie, or any of the "cute" girls he had dated in college. She could well expect and take for granted Dr. Neal's personal respect for her, but she was of another species from which he would never make a selection with which to breed. She had never been a part of his world of graceful, well-groomed people. He could advise her without involvement. Perhaps it was a matter of breeding. Married to such a man, could she trust herself to give a dinner party for his friends, certain that the table was set properly with the right pieces of silver? The linen fresh, the china and serving dishes correct? And could she feel herself relaxed as a hostess, without being nervous and jittery? And when they undressed at night, could she bear the physical intimacy and not be fearful that her undergarments were soiled or her body's flesh too redolent of nervous perspiration, her sexual parts not offensive with female odors? No. She feared that the very sweat that exuded from her body's crevices would give off an odor offensive to a man of Dr. Neal's gentle breeding. Her very sweat would tell him of her life of worry and insecurity and jealousy and heartache. Real intimacy with her, she was certain, would offend him. She was like one of the heifers on her Uncle Andrew's farm that was good enough to give milk, but not to breed with his prize bull.

"I'm giving you some Seconal. It'll help you sleep at night. Also some tranquilizers and some hormone pills. The directions will be on the bottles. Both pills will help to calm you during the day."

"Thank you, Dr. Neal."

"This medication will help you until you see Dr. Rubin. He's a very busy man. It may be a week or more before he can see you. He'll take care of your medication then. Meanwhile, if you get panicky for some reason or other, I'm here."

"Thank you."

"Don't thank me. It's my business to help you and I want to."

She was afraid she might cry again, his matter-of-fact consideration touched her so deeply. "What can you tell me . . . of the seriousness of my condition, Dr. Neal?"

He put the prescriptions into her hand and spoke solemnly, looking closely into her face. "I'm afraid you're undergoing a premature menopause, Miss Wyckoff."

The diagnosis grabbed at her heart like a pronouncement of sudden death.

"But the hormone shot along with the pills will undoubtedly bring you around again."

"But, Dr. Neal, I'm only thirty-five!"

"I told you, it's *premature.*"

"I didn't think it possible . . . at thirty-five."

"As I said, Miss Wyckoff, if we don't use our bodies, they begin to atrophy."

"This is a great shock." And Miss Wyckoff looked white and stricken.

"I hate to see it happen in one so young."

"Yes," she agreed meekly. "I . . . I hope it can be averted."

"It *can* be averted. But now that's getting into Dr. Rubin's field. I don't think I should say any more. I only hope I've not said too much already. Good luck, Miss Wyckoff."

7

It was strange he should have asked her if she had any antagonism to Jews, Miss Wyckoff thought as she walked away from Dr. Neal's office. No really intelligent person, she had always told herself, could hate an entire race of people. Growing up in the little town of Belleville, she had never been aware of any serious prejudice against any minority. There were only two Jewish families in the town at that time, one of the families having a daughter her own age, a friend of Evelyn's. There was such a total lack of prejudice, Evelyn recalled, that the other students frequently kidded Martha Mayer if they caught her eating ham in the school cafeteria. It was the kind of good-natured kidding that almost every adolescent is subject to from his contemporaries, for any noticeably individual characteristic.

Evelyn remembered being kidded for having red hair; blonds were kidded for being blond; bow-legged boys were kidded, and anyone wearing braces on his teeth; the two children of the one Italian family in town were called "garlic eaters." Individual differences were candidly registered by the young and brought into the open, but without any maliciousness of feeling. As for the few Negro children she had gone to school with, they were too poor, as were many whites, to take part as equals in school activities; and so they, unhappily, escaped good-natured name-calling.

There was one Negro family, the Dodges, who were better off financially than most whites, for the father was a doctor and made a good income treating the town's Negroes. Helen Dodge was a student in Evelyn's class in domestic science, where they learned to cook together. Other students were always respectful of the Dodge children, but never took into consideration the unfairness of their not being permitted to eat in the school cafeteria, or mix with white students in the school swimming classes, or sit anywhere in the local theater except in one section of the balcony. If they were allowed to attend the white people's churches, they were not encouraged to, and so attended a church of their own.

Evelyn felt the injustice of the Negro's position in society at a very early age. When she took public speaking, she made many speeches about "equal rights" that were always applauded by the class, and her arguments were agreed with by the other students; but that was before the war, and no social change took place. It was an issue she at times became irate about.

Evelyn didn't become aware of any existing prejudice against Jews until years later when she attended her first summer session at Columbia University, after she had begun her teaching job in Freedom. For a long time, she felt she had to like every Jew she met to avoid the anathema of being anti-Semitic, a term that was, in those early postwar years, being used in accusation of any slightly right-wing Aryan. Evelyn would rather die than be considered a "right-winger." She prided herself on her liberal attitudes as she would on prizes she had won, for she had earned her social viewpoints with the hard work of reason. It was a long time before she realized it was permissible to dislike a Jew personally. Her friend in a class in semantics, Rebecca Horowitz, helped to straighten out her thinking in the matter. She shocked Evelyn one day by referring to an aggressive Jewish student, a male, as being "such a yid."

[85]

"Why, Rebecca, how can you call him a name like that?" Evelyn exclaimed.

Rebecca laughed, "Oh, come off it, Kansas. You can't pretend you like the son of a bitch."

Evelyn thought very deeply. She had to admit to herself, and then to Rebecca, that she did not.

"Look," Rebecca said, "if there's racial equality, we have the right to hate bores and loud-mouths regardless what species they are."

Evelyn was a little reluctant to admit she was right. "He *is* an aggressive fellow, but after all, Becky, any member of a minority is bound to be . . ."

"Now that's *real* prejudice, Evelyn. If you think you have to go around loving all Jews because of what happened in Germany, then you're as guilty as Hitler is, or *was*. For God's sake, respect us enough to hate us when you feel like it."

"I see," Evelyn said in a small voice that held an enormous new realization. "Yes. Of course I see." But if anyone but a Jew had told her what Rebecca had, she would have labeled the person "a vicious anti-Semite."

8

MISS WYCKOFF felt better after seeing Dr. Neal. Now all the vague, nightmarish fears she had been trying hopelessly to cope with were crystallized into one very solid and real fear, of menopause. This fear in itself amounted to terror, but at least it was definable, and she could deal with it. The mere fact that she was going to see the doctor in Wichita gave her a conviction that she was doing something to help herself. Also, the medication helped her. She had never taken sleeping pills or tranquilizers before, and they made the day a little easier for her, facing her students and members of the faculty. Also, it gave her a curious kind of pride to realize that she was going to visit a psychiatrist. Only the brightest, most sensitive people needed to see psychiatrists, she reasoned. She had read in magazines about famous actors and writers who had gone to psychiatrists. There was no longer any cause to feel embarrassed about it. Still, she would mention it most cautiously to Mrs. Heming and Beth and a few of her closest friends among the teachers. And still, she feared that first visit much as she feared the breaking of her hymen.

Dr. Rubin was unable to see Miss Wyckoff for several days. Her appointment was set for five o'clock the following Monday afternoon. She would take the three-thirty bus from Freedom and arrive in Wichita in time for a half hour of window-shopping before her appointment. Given the weekend to indulge her new grief, she took long walks in a woods outside of Freedom. It was a sad but beautiful time of year, when the bright leaves were just beginning to fall, a season that had always made her a little melancholy. But it occurred to her, she had always been happiest when she was just a little melancholy or sad. It didn't seem to her in any way abnormal that this should be. Only a fool could face life with laughing happiness. She could feel gaily happy upon a few special occasions, like having one of her students win first prize in the annual state scholarship contest, or getting a raise, or finding that her oil stocks had risen in value. But this was not a happiness with which to meet the reality of everyday life.

More than melancholy, it was a feeling of bitterness that
she felt about the threatened loss of her sexual usefulness.
She had never used her body as a woman. She had ig-
nored her animal function in life. And she had missed,
undoubtedly, great pleasure, even ecstasy. She felt that
she was being deprived of this usefulness before life had
let her realize its importance. What a loss, she felt, to live
all of life and die without ever knowing the rapture that
another body could make her feel. Her intuitive senses
told her something of what this rapture could be, for she
had enjoyed erotic dreams, and responded to the love
scenes in romantic novels and plays and movies. She could
respond pleasurably to the lusty scenes, too, and the semi-
pornographic in translating Ovid and Apuleius. At times,
lying on her back in bed at night, her face looking up
into the privacy of darkness, she could imagine realis-
tically what a man's body on top of her own would feel
like, a body much bigger than her own, with hard mus-
cles, and thick hair perhaps on the chest, and strong hands
that would fondle her small, firm breasts softly, and full
lips that would press hard upon her own and dart a tongue
inside her mouth for her to suck on, and kiss the stiff
nipples of her breasts, sucking them, as she might kiss
and suck on the man's hard prick, and cup his testicles

in her hand and feel of them tenderly. And maybe, too, he would kiss the lips of her unentered vagina and probe his tongue inside her. Her quick senses told her what ecstasy this would be and she would sometimes finger the lips of her vagina until she felt the pleasure of release from her teasing fantasies.

Of course, convention forbade her using her body to reproduce. She had forsaken the role of motherhood, probably since the days of her early childhood when she would hear and see her parents fighting so vociferously that she would be frightened by them, and sometimes hide in a closet and cover her ears. Two people were not meant to live together in such discord, her child's innate reason told her. She herself would never consent to live that way. There were times when she feared that her father and mother might kill each other, or one kill the other. Did all men and women live together so miserably, she wondered. Could they ever live together without fear and feud? Her child's fear told her no, and her child's mind began to lay the deepest foundation for her future life. She would live it alone. She would work hard and ignore a man's role as husband, and make herself independent of him, of everyone.

But a sexual relationship meant more than the material

product of a child. The uniting of two bodies was one of the most beautiful and thrilling experiences that life could offer to the senses and the spirit. It was the great experience around which most of life revolved. And having been told by a medical authority, Dr. Neal, that her "long-preserved virginity" (she could not help recalling Marvell's ode in her situation) was harmful to her, Miss Wyckoff at the age of thirty-five began to ponder the possibility of having her first "affair." It was a dreaded excitement, but she felt herself determined to have one, to know this greatest of experiences that two humans could share together.

For the first time, she began to think of men and regard them as possible lovers. Their attractiveness was not, like Dr. Neal's, something forbidden her; it was now something to challenge her. But how awkward and ill-equipped she felt herself to deal with the force so new in her life. How could she ever learn to flirt, she who had spent her life in still libraries and chalky classrooms and woman-smelling rented rooms? She didn't expect herself to be an obvious flirt or a tart, and she would hate herself if she ever became coy and giggly around men; but she wondered if she would ever be able to allow a look of longing in her eyes when she faced an attractive man; or if she would ever be able to smile at him in such a way as to grant him privilege, if he chose, to advance with her. These would be difficult maneuvers for one so long trained to exhibit, almost forbiddingly, her independence of men. She felt herself now the inferior of any carefree little high school girl who could laugh with boys and accept their rough hands on her body, and their warm-breathed kisses on her mouth, and not be shocked or frightened by the animal heat of their bodies' closeness.

The first thing Evelyn Wyckoff did when she returned to her room at the Hemings' after seeing Dr. Neal was to take off her clothes and stand naked before the long mirror at her dressing table. She stared thus at herself for five or six minutes as if to evaluate her physical appeal. By now she could take her lovely pink and white skin for granted, and the fineness of her red silky hair and her green eyes, also her well-shaped little hands with their pointed fingers and the trim ankles and wrists. But she was short. Many men liked a small woman, of course, but Miss Wyckoff knew that she was stocky. Diet couldn't help, she was born to be short and stocky. But she was not fat. Still, she would never have the slim, flexible body that had been fashionable ever since she could remember. And her waistline was not much slimmer than her hips. But beauty, she had remembered reading in an article written by some psychologist, was largely in a woman's mind, in her concept of herself. She thought that was very true. Fern Hudson, for instance, naturally thought of herself as beautiful. And even though she did possess lovely features, had she not thought of herself as beautiful or recognized her beauty, probably her beauty would not be so proclaimed. People are inclined to accept us as we offer ourselves to them. Evelyn had never offered herself as a beauty or even as a mate for man. So thoroughly had she driven romance from her life, she had always failed to recognize the little signs of flirtation and physical advances that men had occasionally made toward her. She had not known how to interpret these signs and advances. She met them dumbly and interpreted them as some awkward form of behavior the men had performed unwittingly. From now on, she would try to think of herself as beautiful and attractive to men.

Many women like Evelyn, and in her situation, would have turned to their own sex for sensual gratification, and a few of the other girls living at Slocum Dorm when Evelyn was an undergraduate had made advances to her which she could not fail to recognize for what they were. But she could not respond so to her own sex. In movies and literature, she could allow herself to fall in love with the hero, and to identify herself totally with the heroine when she was swept into her lover's arms for a passionate embrace and an open-mouthed kiss that made Evelyn feel at times the lovers were going to devour each other. But upon finishing the book or leaving the theater, her own world returned to her in which passion and romance were as out of place as muskets and sabers.

On the bus to Wichita to keep her first appointment with Dr. Rubin, Evelyn felt almost giddy. It was almost as if she were having her first date, and her curiosity about the person of Dr. Rubin led her to think of him romantically. Dr. Neal had said he was a Jew. Some Jewish men could be extremely attractive, she knew.

The bus driver was a man she had ridden with before, numerous times on weekend jaunts into Wichita. Recognizing her, he smiled at her and tipped his cap. She had always noticed that he was a good-looking man about her own age, but his good looks had never seemed of consequence before. Now they were. She smiled back at him and gave him a greeting this time, and walked with a little swing in her hips to one of the back seats in the bus. Now why didn't she think to sit in one of the front seats where she would be close to the driver? He might smile at her

again through his rearview mirror, and she might catch
him looking at her legs. It was too late now. She'd think
of it next trip. Certainly she had no expectations of
marriage to the bus driver, who probably was already
married, nor of a certain romance. She regarded him impersonally as a male upon whom she might practice her
new-found femininity. Probably he was a year or two
younger than herself, she thought. His face looked boyish.
And she liked his boots. He must have good legs to fill the
boots so fully. Men's legs could be very beautiful, she now
admitted to herself. A man's well-muscled leg with a slim
ankle was probably more elegant than a woman's. The
driver also had a cleft in his chin. His chin was shaped
like miniature buttocks. No. She was not going to scold
herself for having a dirty mind. These awarenesses she
had were things she should have faced and admitted a
long time ago. It was natural to notice a man's attractiveness. It was not dirty.

Dr. Rubin was not one of the Jewish men who are handsome and sexually attractive. He was a small, thin man in
his forties with an unromantic moustache, and he wore
glasses that neither added to nor detracted from his looks.
He was a scrutinizing man who looked upon her when
she entered as yet another unexplored member of this

curious, unpredictable human race. Any girlish expectations of romance were dispelled immediately when she
felt his eyes upon her. She remembered quickly that she
had come to visit the man because she was ill. And she
liked him. His voice, when he introduced himself, had
an impersonal warmth that seemed to tell her as well
as and more gracefully than any words that he would be
as warm and friendly as the doctor-patient relationship
permitted. But within such boundaries, the entire realm
of human experience could be dealt with, Miss Wyckoff
felt; and something inside herself, some stiff resistance,
began to relax when she sat in the chair before the doctor's desk, and for the first time in many weeks, the tension in her body began to ease and she could feel how
physically tired she was from the long period of anxiety
and morose melancholy she'd been through.

"I didn't realize how tired I was," she said, laying her
head on the back of the chair and easing her feet from
her tight lizard shoes, so close to the desk that Dr.
Rubin needn't see. Women who immediately made themselves at home by removing their shoes at a friend's
house repelled Miss Wyckoff. She permitted herself such
an indulgence now only because she felt she had earned
it. Actually, she now felt herself so tired, so bone-weary,

she would have liked to lie down on the big leather couch on the other side of the doctor's desk and have a long, sound sleep, with her newfound guardian sitting by. Probably the sleep right now would help her more than anything else, giving her the strength to fight her depression. No. She mustn't think of it as *fighting*. The depression was too powerful to fight; she must think only in terms of *dealing* with it.

Dr. Rubin said nothing. He exercised none of Dr. Neal's considerable charm in helping her to feel at ease. Undoubtedly there was some purpose in his appearing so detached. Miss Wycoff's first feeling of relaxation began to leave and she felt the return of tension. If only he would speak. But he wouldn't. The silence was unbearable. So Miss Wyckoff opened the interview.

"I guess Dr. Neal told you, I've been very depressed."

9

MISS WYCKOFF responded well to treatment from Dr. Rubin. But the next few months were painful for her. A semihysterical woman, she would sometimes lose control of her emotions in class and retire to the women's faculty lounge and cry. Her friends among the other teachers sometimes would accompany her to give her a little sympathy, which she craved, and help her to "get hold of herself" once more. At times when they persuaded her to go to a movie with them ("Now, Evvie, come along. If you don't, you're just going to stay home and brood. Now come along, Evvie") she might get suddenly very upset at some sad scene in the movie, maybe a scene that the other teachers didn't find sad at all, and would have to leave in the middle of the picture and go home, where she would sit in her room crying floods of tears.

Perhaps the movie of *A Member of the Wedding* affected her most. The plight of a girl entering adolescence with no certain friends or social ties, with no certain future to grow for, not knowing how she would ever face life or live it, was a dramatic situation that so oppressed Miss Wyckoff, she cried about it for hours that night before finally drifting off to sleep. And the next few days, whenever the picture would come to her mind, the tears would return to her eyes. She of course had made a quick identification with the character of Frankie when she saw the film, and it brought back to her the isolation of her own childhood, which she had been discussing with Dr. Rubin. She could cry now for the lonely little girl she had once been. Heretofore, she had always scorned self-pity, even though she indulged in it whenever possible. And occasionally a piece of music would bring on one of what her friends had begun to call her "spells." One morning at assembly, a gifted singer in town, Mrs. Henry Blood, performed for the students and faculty, singing some of her favorite songs with her talented son Billy accompanying her at the piano. The song that most affected Miss Wyckoff was Rachmaninoff's "The Floods of Spring." She had never heard it before. Its melancholy opened her heart like a floodgate and sent her hurrying out of the auditorium to the lounge, where she stayed for the next class period trying to overcome her compulsive tears. Her friends among the other teachers worried about her, and discussed her often when she wasn't in their company.

"Kid, what *is* the matter with Evvie?"

"She's going through her change."

"But she's so young!"

"I guess that's why it upsets her so."

"Is it true she's seeing a psychiatrist in Wichita?"

"Well, what's wrong with seeing a psychiatrist? Lots of very famous people have gone to psychiatrists."

"Well, I just hope he's doing her some good. I'd hate to see her spend all that money on a quack."

"He's a very good doctor. Dr. Neal sent her to him."

"Poor Evvie!"

"She's too sensitive."

"Her students are beginning to talk about her."

"Well, what if they are!"

"I just hope she comes through it all okay."

"She will. Of course she will."

But if there were bad times during the course of her treatment, there were good times, too. The illumination of a new insight was always a great reward for any agony that treatment had imposed. Dr. Rubin made it clear from the beginning he was not going to subject her to deep analysis, but nonetheless, he put her on the couch and probed sometimes deep into her unconscious, just as Dr. Neal had probed into her body. After a few weeks, he told her he thought he would be able to help her "over the hump" of her illness in a matter of several months.

It was a great learning experience for Miss Wyckoff, and most usually she looked forward to her visits with Dr. Rubin, and sat in the back of the bus twice a week in the late afternoon, her eyes out the window gazing at the level Kansas landscape that she had come to find so much unadorned beauty in. When she first started seeing the doctor, the trees were still in color. Then came December and there would be occasional light snows on the ground and trees. She did not go home to Belleville that year for Christmas but stayed on at the Hemings' and continued seeing her doctor every day during the two weeks of vacation. It was the first Christmas she had ever spent away from home. She had to make up an excuse for her worried parents about having "a lot of work to catch up on." The letter that conveyed this message brought an anxious telephone call from her mother.

"Evelyn, dear, why can't you bring your work *home* with you?"

". . . Because I have to stay here, Mama, where I can use the mimeograph machine in the school office." She had had to think fast to create an excuse this believable.

"Now, Evelyn, you're not hiding anything from us, are you?"

"Like what, Mama?"

"Like maybe a . . . a sweetheart?"

"No, Mama."

"Are you sure?" (Evelyn noticed the sound of worry in her mother's voice.)

"Of course I'm sure, Mama."

"Then are you sure you're not sick?"

"I'm perfectly well, Mama."

"Well . . . your father and I both are brokenhearted that you're not coming home. It's our first Christmas without you, Evelyn, and . . ."

"You'll have Irma. She'll keep you company."

"But we've always before had the two of you. Oh dear, Christmas just won't be the same . . ."

"I'm sorry, Mother. I'd love to come home if I could. But I have to do this work."

"Well, you be a good girl now."

"Yes, Mama."

"And call us Christmas morning."

"I will."

She was just discovering how difficult it can be to break the infant relationship with one's parents, particularly when the parents, like her own, did not know any way to treat their grown daughters except as the children they once had been. How lovingly her mother would have treated her upon her arrival, had she gone home as before. Her mother and father would have come to the train together and Mrs. Wyckoff would have thrown her arms possessively around Evelyn and exclaimed, "My baby! My baby's home again." And her father would have kissed her fondly on the cheek and given her as sincere if less demonstrative a welcome. And they would have put her into the old Oldsmobile and driven her home and showed her into her old room.

"I can't come into this room without crying that my baby isn't with me anymore," her mother would have pouted. Evelyn would be too embarrassed to know how to answer her.

And for dinner that night they would have fried chicken and mashed potatoes and cream gravy, and rich chocolate cake. It was Mrs. Wyckoff's most reliable menu for a homecoming meal.

"Now tell us all about what you've been doing," her

mother would say after dinner, as if expecting her daughter to become a Boccaccio spinning wondrous tales about her life in Freedom.

"There's really not much to tell, Mother. After all, I lead a pretty ordinary existence there."

"Oh, but you've got a sweetheart there. I'm sure of that. And you're just not telling."

"No. No, Mother. That's not true."

"Well, shucks! What good is a man, anyway? I say, you're better off without one. You don't have to ask anyone when you want to buy some new clothes, and . . . you have all the freedom in the world. You're *lucky!* That's what you are. You're a very lucky girl to be earning your own living without a man around to boss you all the time."

It embarrassed Evelyn for her mother to talk like this in front of her father. She felt sorry for her father most of the time. She had never realized when she was a girl how cruelly her mother dominated and emasculated him.

But sometimes her father would fight back. Then Evelyn would be sorry she had given up her vacation to come home instead of going to Chicago for the holidays and seeing some plays or the ballet. But her mother would have cried like a baby had Evelyn made such a display of independence.

Her first morning home, after breakfast, after her father had gone to town to his office, Mrs. Wyckoff would capture Evelyn and force her to listen to all her complaints against her husband, how stingy he was, how he didn't treat her with the same respect he gave to his sister, how she suspected him of "being sweet on" some other woman in town.

"Mother, I don't want to hear talk like this. I'm home for a holiday. I'd like to come home once and see you and Dad happy together. It would make the merriest Christmas I've ever known to see the two of you happy."

"Well, I do *my* part. I stay home all day long and keep house for him, don't I? And cook his meals, and iron his shirts? I've always done *my* duties as a wife, you can be sure of that. I work my fingers to the bone around this house, and what thanks do I get for it?"

Evelyn would never have the courage to tell her mother what a nag and a shrew she was. How well Evelyn remembered her mother telling her when she was a little girl that men were not physically attractive to herself or to any self-respecting lady. And Evvie had held on to this belief all through her growing years. How confused our mores are, she pondered. Our laws, for instance, deal very harshly and vindictively with a man who seduces a child, but there are no laws to deal with parents who so fill their children's lives with sexual fears that they cripple them emotionally forever. At times, Evelyn wished that some attractive man had raped her at puberty.

"It might have been a terrifying experience," Dr. Rubin wanted her to consider.

"But it would have been better than no experience at all," she rebutted, and the doctor made no further reply.

10

AFTER the first of the new year, when classes had resumed and Christmas ornaments had been sadly
removed from the streets and houses of the little towns between Freedom and Wichita, the landscape all through
the month of January was bleak and colorless, the sky like
granite and the earth soggy with frequent rain and melt-
ing snows. It was a landscape Willa Cather had often
described in her novels. Miss Wyckoff found beauty even
in its bleakness. Sometimes she would see a bright orange
and purple sunset through the window of the bus, over
twenty miles or more of flat country. Far horizons were
much more beautiful to her than mountains, which only
got in the way of the sky.

She was always glad to find the good-looking bus driver
at the wheel. The drivers were rotated on the Oklahoma

City to Wichita run, and sometimes she found herself having to make the trip with a heavy-set middle-aged man with a flushed face and a slight nervousness that found its way into his driving, Evelyn thought. His stops were always jerky, and Evelyn never felt at ease with him at the wheel, as she did with the good-looking younger fellow, whose coordination was smooth and who drove the bus with seemingly effortless control. And her frequent trips had started a speaking acquaintance between them.

"Hi, Red!" he'd greet her when she got on the bus. "I'm beginnin' to think you got yourself a boyfriend over in Wichita. Tell him, the money you spend on bus tickets could buy a wedding ring."

Then he'd laugh when Miss Wyckoff blushed. "Don't lemme kid ya, Red. Tell the truth, I dunno how I could make this trip without ya."

And she would smile at him and tell him he was the best driver on the route.

How sweet his rough cordiality seemed to her! And how much more sincere than the trained gallantry of some educated men. She wondered if he was flirting with her. She didn't know how seriously to take his cordial greetings, nor how exactly to interpret the smile that always lighted up his face when he saw her, and the lively eyes that wrinkled at the corners when he smiled or laughed. She wasn't experienced enough to tell if he was really attracted to her or if he was just being good-naturedly friendly. But she always smiled back at him when she greeted him, getting onto the bus, and began to call him by his name, Ed, after he told her to. But she discovered that Wichita was his home and that he had a wife, who came to greet him one day when the bus rolled into the terminal. She was a young woman with bright blond hair, and he took her into his arms and kissed her when he got off the bus. Miss Wyckoff noticed how their bodies folded together in their embrace, bodies that had come to fit each other like pieces of a puzzle. Miss Wyckoff could not help feeling a little pang of rejection when she saw the embrace. "There but for the thoughtlessness of God go I," she said to herself when she saw the young blond wife in Ed's arms, breathing a kiss from his mouth like taking nourishment to her soul.

The next time they rode together, she could not help but show some of the sadness she felt in knowing now that he was married. And Ed could tell that she felt this. He tried to smile at her anyway, and be as humorous as he had always been before. But he was trying now, and

Evelyn could see the effort he was making. Once in a while, a troubled look would cross his face during the trip, and he would look back at Evelyn through the rear-view mirror as if trying to figure her out. Then the following week when they made the trip together, he spoke to her after they got off the bus in Wichita.

"How 'bout a cup a coffee with me, Red?"

"Well, I . . . I really shouldn't. I have an appointment at . . ."

"He can wait a few minutes, can't he?"

"I guess so. Yes. He can wait."

They sat together at the counter in the coffee shop.

"What's your real name, Red?"

"Evelyn. Evelyn Wyckoff."

"Mind if I call ya Red?"

"No."

"Sure?"

"Yes. I rather like it. No one else has ever called me Red. So it . . . makes you . . . *unique* among my friends."

"You're a nice girl, Red."

"I'm really no *girl*," she blushed.

"Well, t'*me* y'are."

"Thank you, Ed."

"Red and Ed. How ya like that? We could be a comedy team."

She forced one of her polite little laughs.

"Sorry about the wife, Red."

Now Evelyn was very embarrassed. "Oh . . . please don't be. Good heavens! It's perfectly natural you should have a wife, isn't it? Of course. I wasn't surprised. You mustn't apologize."

"I apologize 'cause I like you, and because I like you, I think you got a right t'know just how it is."

"Well, of course."

"How 'bout you, Red? You got a husband?"

"No. No. I'm not married, Ed."

"That ain't right."

"Well . . . right or not, that's the way it happens to *be*. I . . ."

"I know. You're a schoolteacher."

"Do I make it so obvious?" (She wondered why admission to being a schoolteacher was tantamount to an admission of sexual failure.)

"Uah! If you're not married. A girl like you."

"You're trying to give me a compliment, aren't you?"

"I guess so. It just seems to me, you're a mighty fine

piece of woman to be livin' without a good husband. Some guys don't know what they're missin'. And I'm tellin' ya this, Red, some of us guys get married when we're young to some hot-lookin' broad just 'cause she's sexy, and then find out after a few years that there's other things a woman might be, besides bein' sexy, that're a lot more important over the long stretch."

"What qualities do you refer to, Ed?"

"Well . . . take a look in the mirror some day, and you'll see."

"Ed . . . what you've said . . . moves me . . . very much." And it did move her. His words brought her close to tears.

"Look, Red. I'll level with ya. I'm not allus faithful to m'wife. I could show ya a good time here some night. I'd really like to ball a first-class woman like you. How 'bout it?"

New emotions were charging through Miss Wyckoff's veins like spring floods forging new channels over dry land. So much blood was pounding her brain, she felt it would burst.

"You're married, Ed. I couldn't feel right . . ."

"Shucks! Take your fun where ya find it. That's my motto."

"I . . . I just couldn't feel right, Ed."

"Okay. But if ya ever change your mind, just gimme a wink, and I'll show ya a good time. I mean it." Then he pressed her hand hard, and took the check and they left the terminal together, Evelyn on her way to Dr. Rubin, Ed on his way home to his sexy blond wife.

I I

MISS WYCKOFF felt a wonderful new pride in herself as a woman when she made her way to Dr. Rubin's office to tell him, of course, of her encounter with the bus driver. She felt she had scored her first success as a new woman. The brief encounter with Ed in the coffee shop proved to her that it was possible for her to attract men, and that she was not too shy to talk with them romantically. Now she knew how love affairs could happen. For some reason, she felt herself a failure for not having taken Ed up on his proposal. She asked herself if she had rejected him out of a genuine feeling of moral disapproval, or if she had reacted again out of fear of making a complete surrender. Perhaps if Ed had been more of a gentleman and had been dressed in a well-pressed suit and fresh linen shirt and well-knotted necktie, and polished shoes, and his hands and fingernails as clean as Dr. Neal's, perhaps then she would have said yes. Yet she felt certain that Ed's unpolished person and rough good nature had been a sure part of his attractiveness. But an affair with him could not possibly have amounted to anything more than an expression of physical desire. She was not in a position to spurn such an affair, for she had come to respect physical desire as much as she respected her appetite for food. And Ed at least could have given her the experience her body needed, the lack of which, if it wasn't for the continued hormone shots, would certainly lead her into premature middle age.

Ed had referred to her as "a first-class woman." This classification made her feel very humble; for she had never been able to think of herself, for some reason, as "a first-class woman." And being unconvinced of herself in such a role, she couldn't help but wonder about Ed's judgment. Maybe Ed would have expected her to be something she wasn't or couldn't be. Maybe her lack of experience would have humiliated her before Ed. Maybe he would feel disillusioned in her. She could not help thinking of Fern Hudson as "a first-class woman" and the type of woman Ed probably thought Evelyn to be. Yet why, she asked herself, was Fern Hudson any more first-class than herself? Just because she was more physically beautiful? Dressed more expensively? Was wealthier? And had had numerous romances? She knew that these qualifications for womanhood were no better than her own. Were not even as good. It was also being a woman, she was courageous enough to remind herself, to stand up for racial integration in the school cafeteria as she had done a few years after World War II. Then Miss Wyckoff had had to take her stand against a townful of frightened taxpayers who saw, in this one move toward equality, a dangerous threat to their daughters' virtue and to their entire way of life. But once the Negroes were admitted into the cafeteria with the other students, and into the school swimming pool, their presence was accepted by almost everyone as perfectly natural and it seemed a foolishness that they had not been accepted thus years before.) And a few years later, Miss Wyckoff had been one of the most outspoken opponents of Joe McCarthy during the Senate hearings on this man's political activities. There were other faculty members and some townspeople who agreed with her and congratulated her on a letter she had been brave enough to write to the Freedom *Standard* after the newspaper had printed an editorial in praise of McCarthy's "Americanism." But at the time (Freedom being

mostly a Republican community), Miss Wyckoff had had
to take her stand against the major part of public opinion
and even risk her job. Even her landlady was for Mc-
Carthy, and was concerned at times that in allowing
Miss Wyckoff to stay, she might be harboring a Communist. But Mrs. Hudson had never been known to express any social or political opinions whatever. Evelyn
didn't hold this against the woman, for it would not have
been in her character as a pampered and beautiful
courtesan to have espoused these same causes as rigor-
ously as Evelyn had done. She was the town beauty and
she had to play that role alone, not confusing it with any
other. But if Mrs. Hudson was indifferent to issues of
wider concern than her own pleasures, she was far from
being critical. She had even spoken to Miss Wyckoff
about her letter in the *Standard*, whose editor, young and
very hotheaded Gordon Riley, was a friend of hers. The
occasion was a P.T.A. meeting which the woman had happened to attend. She had a daughter (beautiful also) in
her third year of high school.

"Miss Wyckoff, I liked your letter in the *Standard*. I've
watched some of those hearings on my TV set, and I must
say, I think that man McCarthy is an awful bully. I don't
like him at all. And don't you *adore* Joseph Welch? I do.

I tell Gordie whenever I see him at the club that I think
he's *mean* to write those nasty editorials. But he just
laughs at me. Honestly, to hear Gordie talk, you begin to
suspect your own mother of being a Communist."

It had thrilled Evelyn to have such a compliment from
Mrs. Hudson. And she was relieved to find the woman so
fair-minded. But beautiful people are rarely vicious, Evelyn thought. Usually, as if physical beauty had some
power to create spiritual beauty, beautiful people had a
sense of justice and fair play. Gordon Riley was a handsome man, but he was little. Evelyn was certain that his
small stature, like Napoleon's, was somehow responsible
for his bitter thinking.

1 2

"ARE you expecting me to give you permission to have an affair with the bus driver?" Dr. Rubin asked Miss Wyckoff that afternoon when she had told him about her "first proposition."

Evelyn realized then that this "permission" was exactly what she had been seeking, and that all this time she had been endowing Dr. Rubin with the same little-girl fears she had had of her father, and to a lesser extent, her mother.

"It's what we call *transference*," Dr. Rubin explained to her. "We go through life transferring the feelings we held as a child for our elders to people in vaguely similar relationships to us in our mature lives."

Miss Wyckoff saw the whole pattern of most of her social and professional relationships then. She realized that she had always reacted to Mr. Havemeyer as a kind of father, feeling proud of herself as a daughter feels proud before her father when she stands up bravely for a moral cause, or even when she defies him bravely. And she saw that she tended to make a mother of Mrs. Heming, feeling she was being mothered when Mrs. Heming would occasionally bring her Sunday breakfast in bed or a light lunch when she was ill. And she regarded Beth with some of the feelings she had always held for Irma, shopping for Beth's Christmas present with the same eagerness to please that she had always felt when shopping for her sister.

"Do you think I'd condemn you morally if you went on and had an affair with your handsome bus driver?"

"No."

"Then do you think I'd pat you on the back if you told me you had gone to bed with him?"

"No. Of course not."

"You're a mature woman, even though you retain some childish characteristics, as we all do, and maybe you're looking for someone to give you permission to do something you want very much to do but are frightened of."

"But why?"

"Well . . . then you'd feel relieved of moral guilt, and if

the little romance should end up unhappily, if you con-
tracted a disease or became pregnant, both of which
I'm sure you would fear inordinately, you would have
someone to blame. And your own sensitive conscience
could remain free."

"... I guess you're right."

"So you see, Miss Wyckoff, if I am to be of any real help
to you, I can't let you put me in the position you're trying
to put me in."

"All right. I won't do it anymore."

"What I want is for you to be able to make your own
decisions with a free will."

"I understand."

"*Maybe* you do," he admitted with reservations.

1 3

MISS WYCKOFF had never once referred to Rafe Collins during the months when she was seeing Dr. Rubin. This was not a deliberate oversight. At the time, she was unaware of any sexual attraction to the young Negro. Besides being a Negro, he was much younger than herself. And whereas she had always condoned marriages and love affairs between Negroes and whites, she had never considered the likelihood of any such intimate relationship between herself and a black man. It was difficult enough for her to think of the likelihood of such a relationship with a white man.

She had felt well enough to stop seeing Dr. Rubin at the end of February. Ed, the bus driver, had left his blond wife after Christmas and gone to California, where he got a job tending swimming pools. Once he wrote a card to Miss Wyckoff that she kept in her desk for a long time, rereading it frequently, it pleased her so: *Hi, Red! This is a great place except for the smog. It can git pretty bad at times. I take care of rich people's swimming pools. I wish Marilyn Monroe wood use my services but she don't. Why don't you come out here and teach school? Your old bus driver, Ed. P.S. Not too old.* She always reread it with a feeling of sadness, and regret that she had been too cautious to accept his offer of showing her "a good time." It was an opportunity gone. A man I might have loved, she told herself, remembering a line from a poem of Whitman's upon hearing of the death of a man drowned at sea. People we can love are few, she had come to realize. Now she would always wonder what the feel of the bus driver's big, solid body would be, and how the pressure of his kisses would feel upon her lips, and how his hard penis would feel stuffed inside her. Maybe they would have found pleasure together only once. Maybe they wouldn't have found pleasure at all; their night together might have turned into a dismal bore or a disagreeable fight, and maybe he would have given her a disease or made her pregnant. But she still wished she'd had the courage to accept his offer of himself. A bad memory would be better than an unfulfilled one.

She had not had much chance to become more aware of Rafe Collins while she was seeing Dr. Rubin. For two afternoons of the week, she had to hurry when her last class was ended to catch the bus to Wichita; and those afternoons she was free, she did her Christmas shopping or went to her room at the Hemings' and signed Christmas cards. And after the holidays, she was usually too eager to get home after school to remain in her classroom to do her paperwork. She had all but forgotten the afternoon after Thanksgiving when Rafe had first come to her room to straighten up and had both annoyed and pleased her with his distracting humming, and his sly, graceful movements around the room that had made her constantly wary of him.

March was coming in like a lion but Miss Wyckoff, in her heart, felt like a lamb. Dr. Rubin had dismissed her, and on her way back to Freedom, she felt so happy she paid no attention to the snow that was falling so heavily she couldn't see out of her window in the bus.

"I won't say you're totally *well* yet, but no one is. I'd say now you're as well as anyone has a right to expect to be in this world," Dr. Rubin had summarized his treatment of her. Then they'd laughed together. She had come to love Dr. Rubin. During the last session with him, he recommended the continued use of hormone shots to delay menopause because he thought, without telling her, that they might be helpful in preventing depression. Also, she continued taking an antidepressant pill called Tofranil, which the doctor had prescribed "just in case . . ." And he had reminded her again that she was still young enough to have a romance and to marry.

One afternoon in early March, after her dismissal from Dr. Rubin, Miss Wyckoff decided to get her paperwork done in the classroom rather than take home an armful of ungraded test papers. She was mentally very alert now and all her teacher friends were commenting, "Isn't it good to see Evvie her old self again?" She was joining them at dinner now, either at the Gibson or the new Chinese restaurant, and all of them together still occasionally fixed dinner in Cynthia's and Mildred's cozy apartment. Cynthia taught physical education for girls, and Mildred taught arts and crafts. The thought had occurred to Evelyn numerous times that the two women were possibly lovers, but she never mentioned this thought to the others; she didn't want to get any stories about them started. But once in a while, one of the teachers would make some unguarded remark such as, "Isn't it wonderful how well Cynthia and Mildred get along together? Really, they

seem as happy as newlyweds." Beth had made such a remark once when five of them were leaving the apartment
together, all in Judith Mayberry's Chevy sedan. Beth's
remark was followed by telling silence. Evelyn could sense
that Beth was beginning to feel she had said something
wrong, but she was wise enough not to add to her remark
and risk making it worse.

After several moments of the silence, Carol Ann Mc-
Cord (home economics) commented that there was a full
moon. Then all the teachers were anxious to support the
change in the conversation.

"Isn't it beautiful!"

"I pity poor Mama now. She always claims her sciatica's
worse during full moon."

"Full *moon* and empty arms . . ." another of them sang.

"Kid, I think it's a desecration for them to turn that
beautiful concerto of Rachmaninoff's into a popular song,
don't you, Marie?" (Marie Klausson was the music
teacher.)

"I certainly *do*."

"Some doctor once told me that when there's a full
moon, they have to keep closer watch on the patients in
mental hospitals than at other times."

"Girl, there *is* something mysterious about the working

of the moon and all the planets," Judith said driving down Plymouth Avenue (named by the group of Massachusetts people who had first settled Freedom just before the Civil War). "Any of you believe in astrology?"

"Oh, I do."

"I do, too."

"I very definitely think there's something to it."

"I'm Libra, what're you?"

"Aries."

"Rats! I think it's all superstition."

"Well, maybe you're right."

And so on. How surfeited Evelyn felt herself to be with the company of other women. When she was in her room undressing for bed, she thought about how emotionally unsatisfying her life was. Conversation when the "girls" got together was always inane, even though, taken as individuals, each of her teacher friends was bright. Why was it that their camaraderie had something of the nature of children's play? There was always something compulsive about their "fun," as if they were determined to enjoy themselves despite the isolated position society had placed them in. Sometimes, Evelyn had to admit, they acted downright *silly*. And Evelyn would feel again her loneliness for a man, her need for a man whose life would be a complement to her own, whose ways would be different, whose conversation would be different, and who would create a different presence in her life. She was bored by the talk of women, the smell of women together in a close room, the smell of their hair and their nervous perspiration that sometimes left their dresses forever redolent of their bodies. The sickening smell of them when they were careless about padding their menstruations. She was tired of disguising her boredom with the superficiality of their conversation. Even a stupid man was concerned with more fundamental things than women were, she thought. And even a sweaty man could smell clean to her for the honesty of his sweat and his indifference about disguising it. More and more, she longed for a man with whom to share her life and her bed. And the hormone shots that Dr. Neal was giving her had awakened a fervent sexual desire that she tried to work off by taking long walks and joining the physical fitness class that Cynthia Mars held two afternoons a week for the women on the faculty who wanted to lose weight. Occasionally she would condescend to bring herself relief with her pink fingers, in bed at night when desire was at its peak. How ironic, she sometimes reflected in bed at night, that fate should find her now in such a solitary and lonely life.

How could she have foretold, in her growing years, that this was what all her studiousness and hard work, her defensive denials even of wanting the life more playful girls enjoyed, were leading to. She could see now, she alone had made the lonely bed she slept in.

Rafe entered Miss Wyckoff's classroom one leonine afternoon in early March when she was again alone at her desk grading papers. His entrance had been as soft and silent as a panther's in pursuit of game on padded paws. But his pursuit was different from a panther's, and he wore a knowing smile on his face instead of an animal's controlled ferocity on the kill. Miss Wyckoff looked up at his insinuatingly smiling face, and immediately sensed that she was his prey. A little shiver of fear went through her body. Why would he smile at her like that? With a smile so knowing, a glint in his eyes that embarrassed her with his superior knowing. But knowing of what, she wondered. He actually behaved as if he had some telling evidence on her that he was in a position to take advantage of. But his greeting was an ordinary one.

"Haven't seen you round for quite a while, Miz Wyckoff."

"Oh! Hello, Rafe."

"Been busy?" He began languorously to sweep the floor.

"Yes. Quite busy."

She returned her eyes to the test papers where they belonged, for they had been quite shocked to see the front of his torso exposed naked by the unbuttoned coveralls. She could not help but feel that he was exposing himself thus on purpose, for some reason. But why? Despite the new confidence her sessions with Dr. Rubin had given her, she couldn't think that Rafe Collins was trying to excite her sexually. Certainly there were enough girls closer to him in age who would be happy to respond to him thus. But Miss Wyckoff had not been perceptive enough to realize that Rafe was just as isolated as herself. Even more so. Evelyn at least had the companionship of the other teachers. But Rafe was totally alone except when on weekends he would visit his mother in Bartlesville. Miss Wyckoff never thought of the possibility of men being morbidly lonely. Only women got that way she supposed, when men were not attracted to them. But loneliness must have been on his mind, for it was the first thing he mentioned.

"Mus' be kinda lonesome for you schoolteachers, huh?"

She thought carefully before she answered, and tried her best to sound matter-of-fact. "What do you mean, Rafe?"

"Oh, I dunno. Seems t'me, none of ya get much fun outta life."

She thought hard again and then faked an answer and a lighthearted tone of voice. "Oh, I guess we manage all right." Then she tried to impress upon him how diligently she was working. But he was not impressed. Maybe she should take the papers home and grade them in her room. But she felt herself fastened at her desk. She was like a bird held captive by the predatory look in a cat's eyes. She felt powerless and hypnotized by this man's animal cunning. Even if she did get up and leave the classroom, he would feel himself victorious over her. Slowly, she was becoming infuriated. How dare he make such personal remarks to her, a respected member of the high school faculty, a woman he didn't know? But the angrier she became, the closer she kept her face to the papers she was grading, not daring to look up at the athlete. Was he deliberately tormenting her, she wondered. And if so, why?

"Folks tell me you done a lotta good fer the black students here. Got 'em equal right t'eat in the cafeteria."

She looked up at him then. Even then his smile was mocking her, as if he were telling her she was a hypocrite for helping Negro students as she had done. She wasn't able to respond to his statement. She was so

shocked by what she saw then that she began to tremble.
He stood a few feet before her desk. His coveralls opened
down to his belly, his hands in his pockets now drawing
the cloth of the garment so tight over his crotch, seemingly unconsciously, his sexual organs were revealed like a
pet animal squirming under cover. His grin grew wider.
His teeth flashed whiter than tile. The smiling arrogance
of his manner was now conscious and proud of the parts of
himself he was displaying. Miss Wyckoff made the mis-
take of staring at the display, just long enough for Rafe
to know that he had made her newly aware of himself.
This new awareness would give him a power over her
she could not combat. She was his own now, no matter
how she might resist, for him to possess and subject to
his every whim.

"I wonder how many you white people really mean
it when you pretend to like us blacks." (Why was it he
wanted to refer to himself as black, she wondered. He
wasn't black. He was the color of a Hershey bar.)

"Rafe, you must leave here at once. This instant." She
could no longer restrain her anxiety. She spoke in a voice
of command but it lacked authority. His expression didn't
change. He behaved as if he hadn't even heard her command, but he did remove his hands from his pockets and

allow the cloth of his coveralls to conceal again his dangling genitals.

"Whatsa matter, Miss Wyckoff? I say something wrong?"

"No, Rafe. You didn't say anything wrong." (The insolence of his affected naïveté was maddening.) She jumped up from her desk now, gathering her students' papers and putting them into a briefcase. "I must go. It's later than I realized." And she started out the door.

"See ya t'morra, Miss Wyckoff." He spoke the farewell casually as he resumed his sweeping, and the sound of his gentle gibing was still a part of his melodious voice.

Miss Wyckoff dashed out of the room and out of the building, and walked with quick, fast steps all the way home, making hurried plans in her mind. She would go to Mr. Havemeyer's office first thing in the morning and demand that a new maintenance man be assigned to her room. She wouldn't give any explanation. She wouldn't need to. The principal would certainly understand that she wouldn't make such a request unless there was an urgent reason for it. She had no desire to make any trouble for Rafe; she just wanted not to see him again. She was still shaking by the time she got to her room. She had some tranquilizers left, so she took two. She wished Beth were home so she could talk to her and get the whole experience out into the open. It wasn't any good talking to Mrs. Heming. She'd express a useless outrage and be unable to give any reasonable advice. She'd probably want to report the incident to the school board and get Rafe Collins expelled from school. Maybe that was the only way to handle the situation, but Evelyn didn't want to think so. She didn't want to deprive any student of his education just because he had been bold with her.

But for some reason, when Beth came home from bowling, Evelyn couldn't bring herself even to mention her experience; and she told Beth she felt too tired to join the girls for dinner, that she'd ask Mrs. Heming if she could fix herself a couple of eggs and then watch *Playhouse 90* on television in the living room. She looked forward to this program every week.

"Would you like me to bring you some ice cream from Jenkins'?" Beth asked.

"Oh yes! I'd love a dish of chocolate ice cream before I go to bed. Thank you, Beth."

Alone that evening, Evelyn thought troubledly about Rafe. It looked obvious even to her own innocent eyes that he was trying to seduce her. But why *me?* Miss Wyckoff could not help but wonder. She was twelve or fifteen years older than the Negro boy, and she knew she was not blessed by beauty and had never been known to possess irresistible sex appeal. Yet she reasoned with herself that she certainly was not *un*attractive, and she remembered the encouragement that Ed the bus driver had given her womanhood. At times she feared some evil in what seemed like Rafe's attempt to seduce her. She could not but believe that he had some motive besides that of mere sexual gratification. And she still recoiled from the shock she had felt at his bold exhibition of himself. How dare he take such a liberty! she fumed. Yet she remembered vividly the display he had created before her eyes, tempting her presumptuously with the sight of his sexual organs, as if knowing that once she saw them she would want their pleasure. It was an ugly, brazen act; and yet it had aroused desire in her, as he knew it would, and she would never forget it.

If Miss Wyckoff felt any intimidation about sexual relations with a Negro (now that she had decided to brave the experience of having a sexual relation) she defied and denied it. Besides, regardless of how society might classify him, Rafe was known to have more white blood in his veins than black. He was the illegitimate progeny of an Oklahoma mulatto woman and a white father who had

abandoned wife and child. Miss Wyckoff liked the idea
of having sexual relations with Rafe to prove to him and
the world (and maybe to herself) that she had no prejudice. But it was more than a little frightening for her to
think of how he might use her.

When morning came, and Miss Wyckoff entered the
school building, she decided not to speak to Mr. Havemeyer, after all. It was a Friday. There was no reason to
act immediately. She'd give herself the weekend to think
over her situation.

Some of the faculty claimed that Rafe had spent some
of his high school years in a juvenile detention home for
all but killing the white father who would not recognize
him. Some insisted it was an orphans' home that Rafe's
beautiful mulatto mother had sent him to, because she had
to work and couldn't provide for him. It was argued by
all, however, that he was a truculent young man, arrogant
and full of hate. Evelyn liked to fantasize that by
treating him fondly and considerately she would eliminate
this bad side of his character, but she wasn't prepared to
take on this responsibility at once. She would remain the
usual half hour when classes let out in the afternoon, and
then she would leave.

Soon Rafe would be relieved of his janitorial duties because he'd have to be training in the afternoons for track. So she really had nothing to worry about at all. She told herself now that she had become terribly concerned about a very minor incident, even though a shocking one, that other teachers would probably dismiss without a second thought. Well, *most* other teachers. Or at least, a great many. But as the day passed, she began to feel a mounting anxiety that she tried to reason away. "But I'm not even going to see him. I'll be leaving the building at three-thirty, just before he comes to clean up my room. There is no reason in the world for me to feel this anxiety. I'm not going to stay in my room anymore to do my home-work until he goes out for track, and Old Man Bowes re-turns as janitor."

But no efforts to reason away her anxiety brought re-lief. The anxiety continued to mount until, by the time the three o'clock dismissal bell rang, she found herself trembling again, and she hurried into the lounge to take two more tranquilizers. She returned immediately to her classroom and somewhat impatiently took care of the few students who had come in to get assignments for makeup work or to hand in late themes. When three-thirty came, she didn't leave. She found herself seated at the desk, grading more papers even though it was hard to concentrate on them, feeling herself as powerless to leave as she had felt the day before. Some force more powerful than her will kept her gravitated to her desk. She finally had to admit to herself, amazement overcoming disbelief, that she could not resist seeing Rafe Collins again. He had been on her mind constantly since the afternoon before, and her dreams that night had been troubled by obvious symbols of coiling reptilian animals that threatened her. And the first thing that came to her mind when she woke in the morning was the contemptuous smile on his chocolate face and the whiter than white teeth. She had to see him again. And after all her protesting to herself that she would never subject herself again to his demeaning presence, she found now that she was impatient that he was not there in her room at the time he usually came, about three-forty, time enough to give the conferring students to leave. And so she waited. And while she waited, she looked out her window at the practice field in back of the junior college and saw that the other track men were already at practice. But Rafe was not among them. It was ten to four when he sidled into her room carrying his broom and a bucket of water and a sponge. Even his walk, she thought, suggested the bodily writhings of sexual rapture.

"Aren't you going out for track this year, Rafe?"

"No'm."

"Oh? Why not?"

"Ligament."

"You mean . . . you tore a ligament?"

"That's what the doctor say."

"Oh. I'm sorry."

"I ain't."

"Didn't you want to go out for track?"

"Not much."

"Is the torn ligament painful?"

"Not much."

"It doesn't hurt you when you're at work?"

"No."

He wore a freshly laundered and starched suit, the buttons of which were open as before all the way to his belly, where the tight belt held the divided garment together.

"When did that happen, Rafe?"

"Few days ago in the gym. It's swollen." Now he moved toward her and took her hand. "Wanna feel?"

His warm brown hand took her pudgy pink and white one and pressed it into the ravine of his groin. She had no will to resist this unwonted intimacy. She let him use her hand thus, dumbly, and remained inscrutably silent as he

pressed her fingertips farther down his groin. She could
not allow her eyes to recognize his use of her hand, and
she stared blankly out of the window while her fingers
felt the firm flesh of this intimate part of him.

"How's it feel, Miss Wyckoff?" he asked in a soft, most
personal voice to which she had no courage to respond.
She continued staring out the window.

"Do you feel the swellin' there? Hmmmm?"

"Yes."

"You kin feel it better bare. Here. Lemme me show
you." And then he drew down the zipper of his fly, putting
her hand inside and pressing it hard against his inner
thigh, the back of her hand feeling the soft, loose genitals.
Neither spoke. Pretense was gone. He no longer tried to
disguise his purpose or desire, but placed her hand around
his thick penis as she had feared he would do.

"That's beginnin' to swell, too," he said in a hushed,
private voice.

She still could not look him in the face, but she mas-
saged the tumescent penis like some long-forbidden object
that she was now daring to let herself know the feel and
texture of. His bold movements, his bold remarks, she no
longer took offense at. She felt a surging of wild emotions, terror, excitement, desire, fear, all of which were

slowly surrendering to his understated domination of her.

"You like what you feel, Miss Wyckoff?"

Still without looking at him, with tears about to fill her eyes, she made her embarrassed admission with the slightest nod of her head. He put an arm around her shoulders. He smelled as clean and washed as his uniform, and his arm felt strong.

"You ain't never had a man before, have ya, Miss Wyckoff?"

His question stabbed her like an indictment of crime or dereliction. She was too transported by new sensations to attempt a lie. She answered him with a simple, softly spoken no. And he grinned, "I knew it." And with her admission, she had given in to his total possession of her.

"*How? How* did you know?"

"I c'n allus tell," he answered with an assurance that was maddening to her but also attractive. Suddenly, it seemed the moment created for her, the moment for her to allow entrance into her private body. Rafe had stirred desire in her, and fascination and exciting curiosity. She had not thought that her first sexual relationship, should there even be a first, would be with a Negro; but she saw no reason why the man's race should matter. Still, she could not herself make the surrender.

"Rafe, you must go! Please! Go now!"

But he still smiled as if assured that her protest was false, a silly pretense of gentility that he had contempt for. He shook his head. "Huh-uh. This is no time for me to go. This is the time for me to stay right here."

And he ambled across the room to the door, locking it with one from the chain of keys that hung from his belt. The corridors of the school were empty now, but he was wise enough to take every precaution against discovery. Then he pulled down the blind over the squares of glass in the door. Miss Wyckoff felt a mounting panic with every movement he made, but watched him silent and fascinated. The room being on the third floor, no one could see in from outside. He walked slowly to her.

"We got bus'nes t'do."

Then he unfastened the belt of his coveralls and let them fall to his feet, stepping out of them, a useless garment to him now. He kicked off his sneakers and stood naked before her.

14

MISS WYCKOFF wakened early Saturday morning, before the sun was up, in a fit of self-loathing, so filled with such tearing anxiety, she didn't see how she could get through the day. The experience with Rafe Collins had left her body and mind in a state of horrible shock. The secret flesh of her vagina was wounded and painfully sore from the young black man's forceful probing into her with an organ that had terrified her when she saw its full size. The only penes she had ever seen were on classical statues. Nature, she discovered, equipped men much more generously than did Praxiteles. She was unable to believe her first sight of Rafe's stony erection. How evil it looked! All desire fled then and she wanted her release from whatever pact existed now between them, a pact to which she had never completely willed herself, anyway. But it was too late. He was determined to finish an act that until that moment had only been insinuated. He was using her fascination and curiosity as grounds for privilege and as proof of her real desire for him, a desire that he recognized whether she did or not. She had even fought him with her hands which he laughingly pinned behind her, murmuring, "Why you fight this way? You know what I'm gonna give. Relax, Miss Wyckoff. I'm gonna *fuck* you, baby. I'm gonna get inside that tight li'l cunt even if you scream your head off. Cause I know you're gonna like it when I get in there, baby. You're gonna love it. You're gonna want this prick a mine ev'ry time you kin get it. Yes you will, baby. Yes you will."

She did scream with his first penetration of her, but he muffled the scream with one hand. She still resisted and there was a scuffle which forced Rafe to pin her arms to her body with his other hand. Her head swam and all went dark with the realization that her will was overcome by this man's physical strength, like that of a tiger. The first insertion made her feel she was being disemboweled and she panicked that he might actually split the lips of her vagina. It terrified her to realize that he was so determined to get his pleasure, he would show no mercy for her pain.

"Relax, baby," he advised her. "Just relax. It's gonna hurt a li'l at first, but if ya jus' relax it'll go in nice and slick and then you're gonna love it. Now, relax, Goddamit!"

The bit of animal wisdom Miss Wyckoff possessed finally came to her rescue and she did relax. She withstood the pain with every inch that he thrust into her, and then she was able to endure his gradual probing until he was free to move up and down, back and forth, inside her, at first very slowly, but later with some ease. Then, very slowly, she could feel the pain convert itself to pleasure, and then he could free her to throw her arms around his shoulders and hold him close to her.

"Now you're learnin', doll baby! Now you're doin' just fine," he whispered to her, and he blew his hot breath into her ear and softly mouthed the lobe. It didn't take her long to reach her first ecstasy, and with it, the moisture seeping down inside her thighs, partly his semen and partly her virgin blood. And then all desire was sated in her and she wanted Rafe to stop and withdraw. But he laughed scornfully.

"We're oney started, baby. I wanna git my rocks off, too. You gotta gimme more time, baby. I din go t'all this work jus' to show *you* a good time."

She thought it would take him forever to reach his own orgasm, but she knew it was useless for her to stop him. Had he treated her with more affection, she might not now be suffering the contempt she felt for herself. But he used her ruthlessly, seeking as much to humiliate her as to give her pleasure, and seeking his own pleasure in her humiliation, in flaunting his maleness and animal superiority over her, and finally forcing her into boldly erotic acts that she had only imagined the practice of. He brought her to climax several times, and she felt a gratefulness to be able to tell herself, "At last it's happened to *me!* At last I know what the experience *is.*" And she had responded at first with rapture, but finally with exhaustion and repulsion. Now she wanted her innocence back. She had to recognize a different woman now when she looked into the mirror. She didn't know if she could live with this new woman she dreaded she might be, a woman addicted to sexual pleasure, for whom serious pursuits lost meaning.

The tranquilizers Dr. Rubin had given her did little now to relieve her panic. (She remembered one of her teacher friends referring to a woman's "penis panic.") She felt now a horror of having been misused and a deep shame that maybe she had wanted to be misused. Desire and repulsion were so fused in her, she could not distinguish one from the other.

Dr. Rubin had told her she might call him if she ever needed him. She felt it would be a soulful release to talk with him now. She called him late that morning and was told by his secretary that he was out of town for a medical convention and wouldn't return for a week. There was no other possible help. She couldn't tell her story to Dr. Neal without fear of incurring his disgust; and she couldn't even consider going to her Presbyterian minister in the hope of finding some absolution of her "sin." She regarded what she had done as a "sin" because she felt she had dishonored her body, and thus she felt mortal guilt. Her "sin" had isolated her from all the people in her everyday life, and she could expect no solace from them. She could admit her "sin" to no one in the world except a psychiatrist, a man who was paid, as priests were paid in former times, to help man find expiation. He was the only man she could hope to find who would be able to regard her behavior, for which she now suffered, totally objectively. And should he be personally repelled by her confession of "sin," it was his professional duty not to express the fact, and to help her regard what she had done, not as a "sin," but as an understandable act of human behavior; compulsive perhaps, but not abnormal. He would help her to reason away her guilt.

The following Monday, Miss Wyckoff left the school immediately after her half hour's duty at her desk to help students who wanted to see her about their work. She didn't see Rafe Collins. But spurning him filled her with more dreaded anxiety than she had felt after allowing his seduction of her. She feared he might think she no longer wanted him because he was a Negro. She feared some evil retaliation by him if she did not see him again.

Tuesday morning, when she opened her classroom at seven-fifty, she found a note under her door. She took it out of its envelope and read: *You be here this afternoon. You be here.* It wasn't signed. It didn't have to be. Her guilt, like a bright student in the classroom, flagging his hand with the answer to the teacher's question before it is even pronounced, told her who the note was from before she opened the envelope. She felt like an animal caught in a snare. Her stomach quaked, turning her breakfast to bile. She taught her morning classes distractedly. At noon, when she met the other teachers for lunch in the school cafeteria, she could not eat, and she couldn't take part in the conversation.

"Evvie, you don't seem yourself today. What's the matter?" Mildred Tweeny had noticed.

"Oh, nothing at all, Mil. I'm just not feeling talkative, I guess."

During her two afternoon classes, her bowels were full of dread mixed with enough damnable desire to keep her in a state of anxiety. She kept telling herself that she would leave, of course, at three-thirty, just as she had done the previous day; but for some uncertain reason, she feared what Rafe might do if she disobeyed his imperious note. She feared she lacked the moral courage to leave. Her own helplessness terrified her, like being in a frightening dream, unable to move. And desire for him teased her nastily. When three-thirty came, she remained seated at her desk. Some of the other teachers looked in and asked if she didn't want a ride home, but Evelyn said no, that she was going to stay and work a while longer. At three-forty, he arrived. There was no spoken greeting between them. He leaned back against the door, locking it with his hand behind him, and drawing the blind down over the glass. Finally, Miss Wyckoff turned her head and looked and said hello. He returned her greeting with a simple hi, and then, still leaning against the door, he began his inquisition:

"Where was you yesterday?"

"I went with some friends to do some shopping. Why?"

"After this, you be here when I come."

"That sounds like an order."

"It is."

"Rafe, I don't think we should expect anything to happen again, such as happened last Friday. We must just forget that."

"You don't wanna forget that. You was crazy for me . . . wasn't ya?"

Miss Wyckoff remained silent. The situation was absurd but terrifying. He had trapped her into a position in which she was helpless.

"Wasn't ya?"

"Rafe, I think common sense should tell us, a relationship like that can't go on."

"Thasso?" he answered, affecting incredulity, sounding a little amused by her pretense of protest, paying it no more respect than if she had sneezed. "Whatsa matter, Miss Wyckoff? Din I have enough to give you?"

Miss Wyckoff had no defense whatever against such in-

solence. It was impossible for her to answer him. Her
mind couldn't conceive any kind of response. She stood
up from her desk and made as if getting ready to leave.
But when she got to the door, he gripped her arm.

"Where you think you're goin'?"

"I'm going home, Rafe. I've a set of test papers waiting there to be graded."

"Thasso?" He still remained leaning against the door as
if to bar her exit. It was clear, he would not brook any
rejection from her. He was as relaxed and self-possessed
as a bandit with a loaded gun, waylaying a defenseless
traveler. When she gathered her personal belongings and
stuffed them into her handbag, she stood at her desk and
faced him. He had casually unzipped his fly and brought
out his tool, and was kneading it with his thumb and fore-
finger into tumescence.

"You're not goin' off without taking care a this, are
you?"

The sight of his penis numbed her. She stared at it.
She couldn't move. His boldness both shocked and excited her. She realized that if she had not felt some
amount of desire (how much she felt was hard for her to
admit) Rafe Collins would never trouble her. But he

sensed her repressed desire for him or he would have not behaved as brazenly as he did. He pointed his prick at her and grinned.

"Want it, baby?"

She couldn't answer.

"C'mon over'n get it," he teased.

She remained as if frozen.

"C'mon, Miz Wyckoff. Don't let nothin' like this go to waste. May be a long time 'fore you see such a nice big peter again. Better come get it while ya can."

She accepted his humiliations, and there seemed something about them that she should have expected.

"Less see ya beg a little, Miz Wyckoff. Beg for it, honey."

"Wh — what do you mean?"

"I'd like to see you crawl over here on your hands and knees and beg."

"I . . . I could never do such a degrading thing."

"Yes, ya could. C'mon, now. Less see ya. Beg fer this, honey. Down on your knees. Beg." He kept his cock in his hand, still kneading it with his thumb, pointing it toward her. "Junior here wants a li'l attention. If you ain't nice to Junior, his daddy's likely to git mad."

This was his first hint of physical violence. She feared

him, and yet she desired him, too. After all, he had performed most gratifying acts upon her own body when they
were together before, giving her a rapture she had never
dared to hope that her body would ever feel. Humbly
and a little clumsily, she sank to her knees.

"Now come t'me, honey."

On her knees, she made her way across the floor.

Thereafter, she was waiting for him when he came to
her room at three-forty. And if he was a few minutes late,
she became anxious and fretted. Gradually, as the physical pleasure Rafe provided her increased, her modesty
and shame decreased, and she learned to use her body in
relationship and coordination with his. She learned and
practiced every means of giving him pleasure, too. That
was all their relationship consisted of, the practice of the
sexual act. They never shared any kind of conversation.
And she began to feel that the sexual act was a release of
Rafe's contempt for her rather than his lust. But she had
come to be just as needful of him as he had so confidently
predicted. She waited for him each afternoon as a hypo-
chrondriac waits for a doctor. A couple of times he was
a half hour late, and those times he found her crying, and
he would comfort her with his always mocking grin.

"There, there, honey. Daddy's here. Daddy's gonna give

ya what ya need. He just got held up a little while 'cause the coach wanted to talk to him in the locker room. But he's here now." And at times he could be very tender and sweet, kissing her all over her body as she cried and moaned in tormented ecstasy.

But his temper toward her was as unpredictable as a madman's. Often he chose to be brutal, physically or psychologically.

"What if I told some a th'other members a the team what a good piece ass y'are, Miss Wyckoff?"

"Oh, no, please! You wouldn't do a thing like that."

"School board'd waste no time gettin' rid a you, they find out."

"Rafe, you have no reason to do me any harm. What's happened between us here is very personal. You surely wouldn't tell anyone, would you?"

"Well, I dunno," he'd grin very slyly, not willing to give up the mean advantage he held over her. These threats terrified Miss Wyckoff.

"Promise me, Rafe. Promise me you'll never tell what's happened between us. Promise me."

Still grinning, he'd say, "Sure. I promise." But his promises never lasted. A few days later he would threaten her again. It might have occurred to Miss Wyckoff that she could threaten him, also, by going to the principal and complaining that Rafe Collins had tried to molest her. Then, whatever story he chose to tell in his defense would sound fictitious. But this strategy never occurred to Miss Wyckoff. People damned by guilt never see the means of their own salvation, or are too afraid to take the role of accuser. Besides, Rafe probably would have been unmoved by such a threat. It could only mean his dismissal from school, and he gave the impression of being totally indifferent to his whereabouts.

There were times, of course, when Rafe chose to brutalize his victim's pasty white flesh, so sensitive and soft. He enjoyed at times flipping her with his belt, stinging the fleshy cushions of her buttocks or her belly.

"Please, Rafe! Don't do that. That hurt me, Rafe. You're not a brute, are you? You don't really want to hurt me, do you? Please, Rafe! Stop!"

15

MISS WYCKOFF'S relationship with Rafe Collins for a period of three weeks during the month of March destroyed whatever peace of mind Dr. Rubin had been able to induce into the woman's life during her months of therapy with him. She began taking heavier doses of the barbiturates that Dr. Rubin had told Dr. Neal he could prescribe for her. And they would give her only a few hours' sleep at night, leaving her more nervous and anxious, she thought, than had she remained awake, tossing in her bed. She lost appetite again and lost considerable weight during those weeks. The loss of weight would have been attractive in her had there not also grown a look of haggard strain on her face.

And although Rafe Collins never did tell any of the

other athletes or students about his many and varied se-
ductions of Miss Wyckoff, it was noticed by some students and teachers, and by Mrs. Heming and Beth, that
something was happening in Miss Wyckoff's private life,
both mysterious and disturbing. Sometimes Rafe would
telephone her at the Hemings'. Sometimes Mrs. Heming
would answer the call, thinking to herself the voice
sounded like a Negro's, but reminding herself that of
course Evvie had Negro students. Yet, when she could not
help overhearing some of Miss Wyckoff's conversation on
the telephone, she began to wonder what the calls could
be about.

"I told you, you were not to call me here, didn't I? . . .
No, it's impossible for me to meet you there . . . Please
don't call me here again. It's impossible for me to see you
away from the school."

After these calls, Miss Wyckoff would be too distracted
to invent any kind of explanation in case it occurred to
her that her end of the telephone conversation might
have sounded to Mrs. Heming and Beth like evidence of
some disreputation in her life. She would run from the
telephone to her room, closing the door; and the other
women in the house might not see her again for several
hours or until the next morning. Beth and Mrs. Heming

had found cause again to hold private discussions about "Evvie."

"Do you have any idea who that man is who keeps calling, Beth?"

"None at all, Mrs. Heming. I'm as baffled as you must be."

"Does she have a gentleman friend that you know of?"

"No, Mrs. Heming."

"You know, Beth . . . I hate to say this, but . . . his voice sounds like a Negro's."

"Really?"

"I told myself at first that he was one of her Negro students calling her about schoolwork, even though his voice sounds older than a high school boy's. And then when I couldn't help overhearing some of the things she says to him over the telephone, I couldn't believe that he was calling her about schoolwork."

"Usually Evvie's very talkative about her troubles and so on. *You* know how she is. When there's something bothering her, she tells a person. But she hasn't given a word of explanation about the calls. And anyone can see how they upset her."

"Well . . . I know that Evvie's a *good* woman. I can't believe that she's involved in anything *wrong*."

"Of course not. Evvie's one of the most straitlaced women on the faculty."

"I'm sure she is."

"We'll probably find out in time that it all has some very simple explanation."

"I'm sure we will."

The only students in the high school and college who had any intimation that there was any kind of personal involvement between Miss Wyckoff and Rafe Collins were the other athletes who worked on the janitor force. Rafe was not doing his work. They had noticed that after he went to clean up in Miss Wyckoff's room, he didn't show up to clean the other rooms he was responsible for until it was almost time for them all to quit work, lock up the building, and go home. Sometimes one of the other men would hurriedly do the rest of Rafe's work so that they could all leave in time to get an early dinner. Contrary to his threats to Miss Wyckoff, Rafe would never have considered telling any of the other men what was happening between him and the high school Latin teacher. For one thing, Rafe was never close enough to the other athletes, not even to the other Negro athletes, to share any confidences with them. He was a true loner. An unhappy young man who had never found life much to his liking, his mal-

content had constructed a barrier between himself and
others back in his childhood. He would have inspired pity
or at least sympathy in other people, had he not been a
man of such imposing physical presence; but it is as difficult to feel these emotions for a man as impressive as
Rafe as it is for tigers. Even wounded, magnificent animals
retain their splendor. There were two other Negro players
on the college team, both of them good-natured, intelligent
and well liked, but they had little to do with Rafe. The
white players admittedly disliked him. He was tolerated
on the team because he was a powerful back, and he was
fearless in making touchdowns, forging his way through
the opposing team's interference with the power that only
deep and intense hate can supply a man; and he was able
to feel this hatred and power by imagining the opposing
team as the world that he faced, a world that was indifferent if not hostile to him, that he could find favor in only
by scoring touchdowns, no matter how ruthlessly, and by
exciting and degrading white women.

Men of physical action do not take pleasure in gossip of
a personal kind. Three or four of the athlete-janitors had
begun to suspect what was happening in Miss Wyckoff's
classroom while Rafe was there with her, but they snick-
ered about it to themselves and never divulged their sus-

picions to others. And their suspicions remained such for a long time, and they would discuss it kiddingly with each other.

"Hey, you suppose that Wyckoff broad is really puttin' out to that jigaboo?"

"Course she is. What else'd he be doin' in her room till closing time?"

"Aw shit! I can't b'lieve it. She's a nice woman."

"She may be nice but that don't mean she don't like a cock up her legs, does it?"

"Well . . . maybe."

"Whatever any of us think about that black sonuvabitch, ya gotta admit he's good-lookin'. There's plenty a white women'd like to get laid by him."

"Yah. Like in England after the war. Man, those English broads went for the niggers more'n they did the whites."

"Jus' the same, I got my private opinion of any white woman'd do a thing like that."

"Look, we don't know for sure that's what they're doin'."

"Don't be stupid. He stays in there an hour or more in the afternoon. A course he's fuckin' her."

And then one day in late March, when the weather was still cold and there was a heavy snow on the ground, the

mystery of what had been happening behind the locked
and blinded door of Miss Wyckoff's classroom was suddenly revealed to others. A shrill scream, loud enough
to be heard by the janitors in other parts of the building, brought two of the young men running to the room
from which the scream had come. The scream continued,
with the sound of a woman enduring unbearable pain, or
torture.

Finding Miss Wyckoff's door locked, one of the young
men opened it with his master key to find Rafe and
Miss Wyckoff, both naked, she trying to escape the pressure of his loins against her buttocks, his arms pressing
down her shoulders, forcing her breasts against the steam-
ing radiator. Rafe withdrew from her immediately upon
being apprehended, and still calm, unruffled, slipped back
into his coveralls and sneakers. Miss Wyckoff began to
cry, her hands over her eyes, unable to face the predicament she had been discovered in. The young janitors then
were all but sickened to see the dark red burns that
striped her breasts. Without speaking, Rafe, dressed,
sauntered out of the room with the convincing appearance of nonchalance. Miss Wyckoff then tried to keep her
bare back to the young men who had both saved and
humiliated her by discovering her with her assailant. They

stood together in the doorway a few moments as if wondering how to help her, but, after a glance of horrible awareness into each other's eyes, they closed the door behind them and walked away, instinct prompting them that even the offer of help or first aid to Miss Wyckoff would be an intrusion into the intimacy of her situation. Their shock kept them in puzzled silence as they walked down the stairs to the basement, to get back into their clothes and go home. Then one spoke to the other.

"Man! I thought I'd seen *every*thing."

"Makes ya kinda sick, don't it?"

Rafe suddenly walked into the dressing room. He still appeared cool and sinisterly amused.

"Three guesses what you cats been talking 'bout."

One of the boys finally answered, "Whatta ya think?"

"Well, lemme tell ya this much, I didn't force her. She's just a cock-hungry old maid 'n I gave her what she been wantin' all her life."

The other two remained silent.

" 'Sides, I'm gettin' outta this two-bit town. I'm goin' to San Francisco. That's the oney place a colored fella as good-lookin' as me kin make it big. All you cats around here are jealous of me."

It was true to an extent; most of the other athletes bore

some jealousy of Rafe, and resentment, too. But his bravado was built upon shame, a deep shame he could not live with. He didn't come to school again. After Miss Wyckoff left town, he left also, and was never seen in Freedom again.

16

MISS WYCKOFF never had her burns attended to. She was too ashamed to reveal them even to a doctor, who would be sure to ask, just out of simple curiosity, how she had incurred them. She bought an ointment that relieved the pain and helped to heal them. But the flesh on her breasts was still sore as she sat on the footstool in Mrs. Heming's living room waiting for her taxi. The last year or so of her life in Freedom had reeled through her mind like one of the foreign movies (maybe one directed by Bergman or Antonioni) that occasionally came to Freedom and baffled the citizens.

She felt her shame and embarrassment now only when she saw herself in the eyes of others, her friends, when she saw them try to cope with their conflicting emotions, unable to associate the Evelyn they knew or thought they knew with the Evelyn who had taken part in a sordid relationship with Rafe Collins. Evelyn realized that in the great world outside of small-town schools and homes and institutions, her "scandal" would be considered merely idiosyncratic. But she didn't know how to gain passport into that bigger world, nor how she could survive there.

She no longer wasted any regrets on what had happened between her and Rafe, any more than she would regret an accident or illness that she could see was inevitable. She could even feel grateful to Rafe for giving her the experience of being used. If she had also been misused, it was the fault of her innocence, which had to be destroyed. The gentle flirtations of the bus driver had failed to persuade her. Maybe Rafe Collins was the only man strong and stubborn enough to break down her resisting will.

For the first time in her life now, Evelyn realized how a human being is totally alone in the universe. It frightened her to realize that all her friendships up until this time, during the ten years she had taught in Freedom, had depended upon the status of her relationships with her friends and associates, a status that had been destroyed overnight and left her a broken and solitary woman. Still sitting on the footstool, she watched mental previews of what the rest of her life would be, and re-called a sonnet of Edna St. Vincent Millay's that, even when she read it as a young girl, had seemed to have some special meaning for her, as if the sonnet then pre-dicted her own future, already known by her subcon-scious:

> *I see so clearly now my similar years*
> *Repeat each other, shod in rusty black,*
> *Like one hack following another hack . . .*

She knew for a certainty now that she would always be alone, that she would never marry. She bore the smell of aloneness in her armpits. Close to forty, her life was prob-ably more than half over, and what years were left could hardly be meaningful, or joyous, or even pleasant. More of the sonnet returned to her:

> *I see so clearly how my life must run*
> *One year behind another year until*
> *At length these bones that leap into the sun*
> *Are lowered into the gravel, and lie still . . .*

And who would there be to care for her when she became aged and ill? And what specific torture was old age holding for her? Cancer? Arthritis? Heart disease?

But she mustn't try to forecast her future now, feeling as hopeless as she did. When one is grieved and cheerless, one can see the future only as a continuation of the present (Miss Millay had written many happy sonnets too), without allowing for the possibility of a sunny day after weeks of dismal gloom. And she should feel braver now for having faced her aloneness. Maybe she would be a stronger woman now. No one can be called *strong*, she thought, who has never faced the world's precarious hostility.

From upstairs, Miss Wyckoff could hear the sounds of fast little footsteps going from Beth's room to Mrs. Heming's. Then there were soft whisperings before the footsteps entered Mrs. Heming's room and the door was closed after them. Then the whisperings became even softer. The intuition of the condemned told Miss Wyckoff that the two women were discussing her, perhaps wondering whether they should appear to say goodbye. It was no longer important to her whether or not they did, but it would be a little comforting if one or both of them should decide to put in an appearance now at the last minute.

Outside, the taxi drove up in front of the house and stopped and the driver sounded his horn. It was twenty minutes until train time and the station was only a few minutes' ride. But she might as well do the rest of her waiting there. She hoped there would be no one at the station who knew her. Her muskrat coat over one arm that also held her handbag, she picked up her suitcase in the other hand and started for the door when she heard Mrs. Heming's voice.

"Evelyn! Evelyn! Wait a minute, dear."

Mrs. Heming was hurrying down the stairs in a new garment Mr. Heming had given her at Christmas. She had proudly told Beth and Evelyn it was called a "hostess gown." Her cheeks were tear-stained and the sound of her voice was choked.

"Evelyn, I've got to say goodbye."

Evelyn waited impassive at the door. Mrs. Heming, once she was down the stairs and looking at Miss Wyckoff in the face, approached her slowly, almost cautiously, her mind trying to give structure to what she wanted, seemingly desperately, to say.

"I'm terribly sorry, Evelyn." Those were the only words that found their way out of her tight throat.

"Thank you, Mrs. Heming."

"I . . . just want you to know that I . . . well, I'm still your friend . . ."

"Thank you."

". . . and good luck!"

The taxi tooted its horn impatiently. Evelyn thanked her ex-landlady again and went out the door as Mrs. Heming stood in the doorway and watched her departure.

"Good luck! Good luck!"

Thanks, Miss Wyckoff thought, getting into the taxi. *I'll need it.* The driver was an old man she had never seen before. He had got out of the car to help her with her luggage. There was an impersonality about his manner that she was most grateful for. Probably he was an old farmer who had had to come to town to make a living and did not recognize Miss Wyckoff or even know who she was. She began to relax as soon as she sat down in the back seat, even though the sounds of the words *good luck* had begun to seem ominous to her. Usually the words were used to express the most commonplace sentiments that accompany a farewell. But Evelyn had come to realize now that the words expressed their speaker's anxiety

about her. For what else could anyone reasonably wish
her but *good luck? Good luck* constituted her only hope
for the future. Wherever she went, whatever she did, she
would need lots of it.